"Evan?" Chris said.

He put a finger to his mouth, signaling that she needed to be quiet, and backed her against a wall. He grabbed both her wrists and raised them over her head. Then he lowered his mouth to hers and kissed her till her knees felt weak.

When she was able to come up for air, she whispered, "Wh-what are you doing?"

"Kissing you, with the intention of doing a lot more," he answered in a sleepy, sexy voice.

"Now? Here?"

"Now and here. In a dressing room in the middle of the day." He smiled. "You asked what you could do for me. This is it."

WHAT ARE *LOVESWEPT* ROMANCES?

They are stories of true romance and touching emotion. We believe those two very important ingredients are constants in our highly sensual and very believable stories in the LOVE-SWEPT line. Our goal is to give you, the reader, stories of consistently high quality that may sometimes make you laugh, sometimes make you cry, but are always fresh and creative and contain many delightful surprises within their pages.

Most romance fans read an enormous number of books. Those they truly love, they keep. Others may be traded with friends and soon forgotten. We hope that each LOVESWEPT romance will be a treasure—a "keeper." We will always try to publish

LOVE STORIES YOU'LL NEVER FORGET
BY AUTHORS YOU'LL ALWAYS REMEMBER

The Editors

UP CLOSE
AND
PERSONAL

DIANE
PERSHING

BANTAM BOOKS
NEW YORK · TORONTO · LONDON · SYDNEY · AUCKLAND

UP CLOSE AND PERSONAL

A Bantam Book / August 1995

LOVESWEPT *and the wave design are registered trademarks of Bantam Books, a division of Bantam Doubleday Dell Publishing Group, Inc. Registered in U.S. Patent and Trademark Office and elsewhere.*

If you would be interested in receiving protective vinyl covers for your Loveswept books, please write to this address for information:

Loveswept
Bantam Books
P.O. Box 985
Hicksville, NY 11802

ISBN 0-553-44459-X

Published simultaneously in the United States and Canada

Bantam Books are published by Bantam Books, a division of Bantam Doubleday Dell Publishing Group, Inc. Its trademark, consisting of the words "Bantam Books" and the portrayal of a rooster, is Registered in U.S. Patent and Trademark Office and in other countries. Marca Registrada. Bantam Books, 1540 Broadway, New York, New York 10036.

PRINTED IN THE UNITED STATES OF AMERICA

OPM   0 9 8 7 6 5 4 3 2 1

PROLOGUE

My God! My children will be orphans.

That was the first thought that ran through Chris McConnell's head as the teenager with the frightened eyes held a gun to her temple. She had no thought of praying for help, nor did her life flash quickly before her. She worried only for the safety and well-being of her fatherless children if she were killed.

The maternal instinct at its most primal.

Which was why, after hours of a standoff, the tying up and terrorizing of innocent people, including one poor elderly woman who was suffering a diabetic reaction; after listening to loud drug-induced demands for cash and escape vehicles and media attention; after being singled out, roughed up, and threatened with all kinds of sexual violence, Chris—keeping that thought of her children uppermost in her mind—began to talk to the gunman. And talk. And talk. She was a schoolteacher and she knew how.

Which was how she was able to get him to relax his guard just enough so that she could sweep her arm up, knock him on the wrist, and send his gun skittering down the aisle of the convenience store.

Which allowed the army of law enforcers who had been hovering at the door, weapons aimed, to come in and take charge. After they slapped cuffs on the kid, they untied the three other hostages, who had been bound and gagged and stuck in the storage room. The old woman was loaded into an ambulance, and Chris breathed a sigh of relief.

Then the press descended upon her.

Chris kept her hand in front of her face as the cameras exploded, but it didn't matter. She was immediately declared a hero. It was a slow news day, she would say later, no Middle East handshakes, no volcanos or earthquakes, no government scandals. Not even any juicy celebrity gossip. So "Mother of two outwits dangerous gunman, saving three lives!" led off the six o'clock broadcast of the *Denver Action News*.

Which caused her story to be picked up on the wire services, followed by reporters stalking her home for days; also offers to appear on *Sally Jessy Raphael* and *Geraldo*, not to mention a "Crime in the Nineties" edition of *Nightline*.

She'd refused to talk to the press and turned down the television shows, but a week after that terrible night they were still after her. In the past seven days she'd been inundated with more calls and letters than any ten people received in their lifetimes, and had pretty much stayed holed up at home to avoid the tabloid reporters camped on her doorstep.

Marla Simone had called from Los Angeles, pushing and prodding and nagging Chris all that week to at least "take a meeting" with her. Marla wanted to buy the rights to her story and turn it into a TV movie, starring Marla herself, of course. Chris had said no several times, but Marla was nothing if not persistent, and had agreed to stop pursuing Chris only if she would agree to a visit, one on one, in person, from her.

Which was why, as Chris could plainly see out the front window, Marla was now marching up the walk to her home.

ONE

Patting her hair into place, Chris gazed around the small, neat living room while she waited for the doorbell to ring. She was nervous, she admitted it. Not only was she still suffering some jitters from her experience, but it was an uncommon occurrence in Loman, Colorado, to have a well-known actress like Marla drop by for a chat.

Although expecting the sound, Chris jumped at the shrill clanging of the doorbell. Swallowing, she let another ring go by so as not to seem too eager. Then she stood tall, wiped her traitorously damp hands on her skirt, and opened the door.

Yes. It was really and truly Marla Simone—those famous green eyes, that full head of thick black curls, the long, swanlike neck—in person on her front porch.

But she was smaller, shorter than Chris had imagined. Even with the very high red heels on her feet, Marla's eyes barely reached Chris's chin, and Chris was only of average height. A red silk blouse under a pale coral suit made the actress seem both businesslike and sexy at the same time, a petite bundle of steel.

Marla wasn't alone. Behind her, still on the walkway leading up to the porch, stood a man. In the brief glance Chris gave him, she took in the fact that he was quite tall, and his very long legs were encased in snug, faded jeans. He wore a comfortable-looking tweed sports jacket over a black T-shirt. Late thirties, maybe, and rugged-looking, his longish dark brown hair was flecked with gold. He sported a deep tan, and wore mirrored aviator-style sunglasses.

His hands were tucked into the rear pockets of his jeans and a lit cigarette dangled from the corner of his full, sensual mouth. A taller, older version of what James Dean might have looked like had he lived.

In other words, a knockout.

Chris just had time to catch her suddenly absent breath and wonder who the stranger was, when Marla began her assault.

"Chris? Chris McConnell?" A small, slender hand with lacquered nails reached for hers. "I'm Marla Simone."

Wiping her palm quickly on her skirt once again, Chris shook Marla's hand, offering a smile of welcome to her famous visitor. "Ms. Simone."

"Marla, please," the other woman answered in her signature high whisper that managed to be sweet and intimate at the same time. Before Chris could ask her in, Marla swept through the door, leaving a trail of expensive scent in her wake.

The man remained just where he was, his mouth

curving upward in an amused smile that formed long, interesting creases on his face. Leaving one hand in his back pocket, he brought the other around and took a drag on his cigarette. He exhaled the smoke into the crisp autumn day, held the cigarette between his thumb and forefinger, and nodded. "Hi," he said.

"I'm sorry," Chris said, "I don't know who—"

"Oh, that's Evan." Marla's voice came from somewhere behind her, and Chris turned around to see Marla inspecting the family pictures on the fireplace mantel. "Evan Stone. He's a writer-producer. My partner on this project."

"I see," Chris murmured, and turned back to the man whose presence was both unexpected and unsettling. "Well, Mr. Stone—"

"Call him Evan." Her heels clicking on the wooden floor, Marla returned to the doorway and beamed all the force of her larger-than-life personality on Chris. "That way we can all be on a first-name basis, can't we?"

Chris couldn't help smiling back, and it struck her as strange, extraordinary, really, that *the* Marla Simone was standing in her living room and they were grinning at each other like long-lost buddies.

"Why are you still out there, Evan?" the actress called out with a hint of impatience. "Come on in."

"Manners, manners, Marla," Evan drawled in a sleepy, sexy voice that spoke of too many cigarettes and too many bedrooms. "You don't just plow into someone's house without being asked."

"It's all right," Chris said. "Please come in."

His head shifted slightly so that he was looking at her.

At least she thought he was; the sunglasses revealed nothing of what was going on behind them. Taking another drag on his cigarette, he ambled toward her, all easy, self-confident male grace. Maybe not James Dean, she amended. Taller. Less sullen. A young Clint Eastwood.

His scuffed boots made a loud thumping noise on her porch. Then he stood in front of her, forcing Chris to raise her head. He was several inches taller than her, and she noted the fine, straight nose, the chiseled jawline, and the hollows just under his cheekbones.

She also sensed a restless impatience—anger? intensity, for sure—brimming just beneath the understated, almost languid surface of this man. Whatever was going on inside him, his impact on her was immediate, and she felt the breath whoosh out of her body at his nearness.

This kind of reaction to a male presence was not even close to an everyday occurrence for her, and she figured she'd better do some fast subject-changing before she began to slobber on the poor man. "I'm sorry," she said, praying her voice sounded normal. "I'm afraid you can't bring that in here."

"Bring what?"

"Your cigarette."

He glanced down at his hand. The corner of his mouth quirked up slightly. "Ah, a smoke-free environment." He shrugged. "No problem. I'm trying to quit."

Chris followed the movement of his angular, tight body with her eyes as he leaned an elbow against the doorframe, bent his knee, and ground out the cigarette on the sole of his boot. His hands were large, with broad, callused fingers—not the hands of a Hollywood producer or writer, but of someone who did physical labor.

He held up the now-deceased butt. "Would you like me to bury this in your flower garden?" he drawled.

"I'll take it."

While Chris held the cigarette by the filter as though it were a dead mouse, Evan crossed the threshold and sauntered into the living room. She caught a whiff of tobacco as he passed her, mixed in with a hint of lime aftershave; it was not at all unpleasant.

As she was closing the door, she noticed that old Mrs. Crane across the street had parted her curtains and was watching all the activity on the porch with avid enthusiasm. Wonderful. Before the day was out, the whole town would know of her visitors.

"I think your coming here has started up the Loman rumor mill," Chris said ruefully, shutting the door firmly behind her and making sure the curtains were pulled closed. It cast the room in shadows, but that was better than the whole population of Kenmore Street peering in. "And I just got rid of all the reporters. Ah, well, can't be helped. Please, both of you, sit down. I've got coffee in the kitchen. Would you like some?"

Marla clicked on a lamp, then gazed eagerly around the room. "This is perfect, isn't it, Evan?" she said as though Chris hadn't spoken. "Look at the darling pictures on the wall. Little landscapes. And that chair, with that sweet needlepoint pillow. And the matching footstool. Charming. We need to reproduce it just as it is."

Darling. Sweet. Charming. Chris bit back a sarcastic retort. Was Marla even aware of how condescending she sounded as she reduced everything in the room to labels? Maybe it was a sort of film-world shorthand, she thought, trying to give the actress the benefit of the doubt. "Quaint" would be the probable verdict. "Classic small-town America." Which, of course, it was. On the surface.

"Do either of you take anything in your coffee?" Chris asked.

"How about something stronger," Evan replied, that slow drawl of his sounding as if he were requesting something faintly lewd.

She swallowed the urge to giggle. Oh, Lord, she would have to watch herself. "I think we have a little wine left over from last Christmas eve. Maybe a beer or two. That's it, I'm afraid. This is my mother-in-law's home and she's pretty much of a teetotaller, so—"

"Mother-in-law," Marla interrupted, looking up from inspecting the fabric of the maroon drapes. "Aren't you a widow? Husband died in tragic plane crash? You're not remarried or anything, are you?" she went on as though she weren't sure if that was or was not a good thing.

"No, I'm not. My late husband's mother, I meant. This is her house. My children and I live with her."

"Two, right?" Marla's eyes gleamed in the lamplight. "A little boy and a little girl."

"You've done your homework."

Marla nodded. "And you all live here together, right? The father-in-law too?"

"No." The sudden sadness that always came at the thought of Joseph McConnell's death overwhelmed her for the moment. "He's gone now," Chris said quietly.

"So . . ." Completely oblivious of what Chris was

feeling, the actress began to pace back and forth slowly, her index finger on her mouth as she thought aloud. "Three generations in one house. Maybe some friction on how to raise the kids—older morality and newer . . ."

She looked over at Chris, her eyes narrowing speculatively. "No. She's not the feisty type, is she? But maybe we could do something with the two-women-in-one-home thing. Two authority figures. What do you think, Evan?"

Chris was deciding whether or not to inform Marla that the word feisty was usually applied to an agitated terrier, when Evan spoke. He was leaning against the mantel, his arms crossed over his chest.

"I think," he said, "it would probably be a good idea not to talk about Mrs. McConnell as though she weren't in the room. And"—he shot a look over at Chris—"a beer will be fine. Thanks."

Chris felt a small dart of gratitude for the way Evan had picked up on her discomfort and come to her defense. Then she realized she was still holding the cigarette between two fingers and wondered if she looked as foolish as she felt. "One beer coming up," she said brightly. "Ms. Simone . . . I mean Marla . . . coffee?"

"Sure." Marla's reply was distracted as she continued to walk around the room. "Thanks. Black."

"I baked a fresh batch of cookies, if you'd like some."

Marla stopped pacing and beamed a smile at her. "Of course you did."

Chris's jaw clenched a bit more at Marla's obvious

assessment of her: a nonfeisty, cookie-baking home-maker. Like the living room, she'd been labeled quaint.

"I'm told even people in Los Angeles bake cookies once in a while," she said dryly, cocking one fist on a hip. "In between the orgies and the power lunches, of course."

A moment passed, then Evan chuckled softly. Chris's head turned at the sound. He was looking at her, that small, amused smile creasing his face again. "That's telling her," he said.

"Do you have eyes?" she asked abruptly.

"Pardon?"

"I can't see you behind those sunglasses. It's kind of creepy trying to make eye contact with mirrors."

After a pause Evan whistled softly and glanced over at Marla. "Surprise, surprise. I have a feeling Mrs. McConnell has a little more backbone than you figured she did. Am I right?" he added, turning to Chris and removing his sunglasses.

Oh, Chris almost said aloud when she saw his eyes. They were a startling turquoise color with sun and laugh lines radiating out from the edges. Even slightly tired-looking as they were now, his eyes were as wondrous, as sexy, as mesmerizing as the rest of him. Chris had to stifle the urge to tell him to put the sunglasses back on. The mirrors had been less distracting.

"I have my share of backbone, I guess," she said. "And then again, I'm told the words 'stubborn' and 'pigheaded' could have been invented with me in mind. It depends on the circumstances."

She turned abruptly to Marla. "So, coffee and cookies

coming up." Darn. Now she probably sounded a bit too hearty, but it was the best she could do. "And one beer."

She almost ran into the kitchen, afraid that the sudden color that had taken over her cheeks would be apparent to her guests, even in the shadowed light of the living room. Once there, she leaned against the kitchen wall and expelled a breath. Oh, dear, she thought. How could she? Practically panting after a man with a pair of Paul Newman eyes—a stranger, for heaven's sake!—like some teenager. While Marla Simone looked on!

Marla, who for many years was little Debbie on *The Family Finch*, had grown up in the public eye. Chris had grown up with her, watching Marla go through baby fat and braces, her first bra and her first date.

Chris's own childhood—years of a fierce, often desolate struggle for survival—had been diametrically different from the warm and toasty world of the Finch TV clan, which was probably why she'd been drawn to the fictional family, most especially the character played by Marla. Also, as Chris and the actress were the same age, twenty-eight, it was hard not to feel friendly toward her, familiar even.

She would have to be wary of assuming an intimacy that didn't exist, she told herself firmly. The actress wanted something from her, something Chris had no intention of letting her have. She would *not* allow Marla to turn the spotlight on her life. Chris's reasons for wanting to keep her past private might not be that big a deal to someone else, but they were her own business and no one else's.

But it wasn't really Marla she was worried about,

Chris thought as she assembled a tray with coffee cups, a beer, and a doily-covered plate full of walnut cookies. It was her reaction to Evan that was throwing her. *He* was a producer and writer? The kind that she read about in *People* and Liz Smith? Ponytails, trendy clothing, all the best tables at the best restaurants. But Evan, with his strong, weathered face, his long legs and scuffed boots, looked as though he'd be more at home on a horse, riding through one of the ranches that surrounded Loman.

Of course, no rancher had ever affected her the way Evan did. Chris's smile turned to a frown. This instant fascination, this . . . turned-on feeling, was so unlike her. That Evan Stone, a stranger from a very strange land, should walk up her driveway and move her this deeply was as shocking as laughing in church. And equally inappropriate, especially in Loman. It was a good thing he would be riding off into the sunset before day's end.

As soon as Chris said no to Marla.

"What do you think, Evan? Will she go for it?"

Evan lowered himself onto a comfortable-looking armchair and eased his legs out in front of him. His head hurt. He'd been up pretty late the night before, viewing the dailies from a project whose first-time director was twenty-two. Evan had had to point out the problem areas to the kid without destroying his ego. Tricky stuff, especially as Evan tended to be more blunt than diplomatic by nature.

Then he'd dragged himself out of bed at an ungodly hour this morning, boarded a plane to Denver, listened to

Marla yakking her enthusiasm nonstop into his ear, seen to the car rental, and trekked a couple of hours to this town that looked like a set for a Depression-era Capra film and reminded him way too much of his own childhood. None of these activities was on his list of the ten best ways to experience the joy of living.

"Will she go for it?" Marla asked again.

He shrugged. "Beats me."

"The hair's perfect," she enthused, picking up a framed snapshot of Chris and two young children and staring at it. "Off the face in a French braid. I like it—nononsense and feminine at the same time."

Evan let Marla's monologue wash over him as his gaze wandered around the room, taking in the modest side tables, the braided area rug near the fireplace. The furniture was not quite antique quality, not yet Salvation Army. But it was an old person's room, and certainly didn't reflect the sense of life, of *light*, emanating from the McConnell woman.

Marla fluffed at her luxurious curls. "I'll probably wear a wig. Or maybe dye it and get hair extensions. Marla Simone goes blond. What do you think?"

Evan closed his eyes and leaned back. "Sure, Marla, whatever you want."

There was no way Marla would ever look like this Chris person. Natural. Nice. A word he probably hadn't used in years. Marla was an actress and could imitate nice, but not really be it. She was too ambitious, too much a child of show business to ever get back to nice.

Perching on the arm of Evan's chair, Marla leaned casually against his shoulder, forcing him to shift his weight to the chair's other arm. She had a way of hanging on people that was annoying.

"I really want this, Evan," she said in a low voice. "I mean, *really*."

"I hear you."

While Marla babbled on, Evan found himself picturing Chris's face. It was a very agreeable face, one without a lot of makeup. It had been a long time since he'd seen a woman who wasn't shadowed and penciled and contoured to death. And she had a sense of humor. Sharp. Dry. Sardonic. More sophisticated than he'd expected. There was a brain at work.

"I wonder where the rest of the family is?" Marla said.

"At the park," he heard Chris say. "The kids, that is."

Evan opened his eyes to see her setting a tray down on the scarred wooden table. He wondered if Chris knew how terrific that voice of hers was—low and husky, with a honeyed rasp that could curl around a man's nerve endings like brandy on a cold night.

"Where's your mother-in-law?" Marla asked sweetly.

"At the Elks."

As she moved the tray, Chris brushed Evan's knee with her knuckles, causing a small tremor in the skin beneath his jeans. Surprised at his body's reaction, he sat up straighter and leaned forward, wanting somehow to be a little nearer to her. Marla slid off the arm of his chair and settled herself on the adjacent couch.

"It's her weekly bridge game," Chris went on. "And nothing keeps Dora McConnell from her weekly bridge game."

Evan could feel his brain and body stirring to life, his

exhaustion fading rapidly. The coffee smelled terrific. Hell, Chris smelled terrific—lemon and vanilla and a hint of baby powder. He studied her profile while she poured coffee into two flower-patterned china cups, then opened a bottle of beer for him.

She had wide-set gray eyes and a small, up-tilted nose. Her high cheekbones were emphasized by the way she wore her ash-blond hair—its natural color, he'd take bets on it—in a braid that reached just past her shoulders. She dressed like a midwest mom straight out of central casting —cotton blouse, denim skirt, loafers. But he noted the firm, high breasts, the small waist, the long legs.

There was an air of tension about her. Was she always like that, he wondered. Or was she awed by Marla's presence? Or, more likely, still shaken up by her near death experience a week ago? He wanted to know the answer.

Beneath the tension was subtle sensuality, all the more provocative for how little of her body was revealed by her clothing. Evan felt his own body tightening as he assessed her.

"I'm sorry your family isn't here," Marla said as Chris handed her a cup and saucer. "I would like to have met them. To, you know, get a feel for the kind of life you lead."

Chris's only response was a small, tight smile. She handed Evan his beer and he took a swig, then set it down on the lamp table next to the chair so he could go back to studying her.

"Maybe some other time?" Marla persisted.

"Probably not." Chris settled herself on the other end

of the couch, coffee cup in hand. "I can't imagine you'll ever want to come to Loman again."

"I will if we do your story."

"But you won't be doing my story," she said pleasantly enough, then took a sip of coffee. "I thought I made that clear over the phone."

"Well, of course you did," Marla said, nibbling at a cookie, "but that was only the first pass. These are delicious, by the way."

Chris smiled at Marla's blatant flattery. "Thank you. The first pass," she repeated. "As in 'let's take another pass at it?' People in Hollywood really say that?"

"Exactly. No one takes the first no seriously," the actress explained.

"I see. Well, at the risk of sounding ungracious," she said evenly, allowing just a hint of steel into her tone, "consider that the first—and last—pass. I am truly not interested in you dramatizing my life. No matter what you say or how you say it. And I won't be changing my mind."

Evan leaned forward in his chair, resting his elbows on his knees. "Why?" he asked.

He startled her with his question; so far he'd been the observer, Marla the talker. After a sip of her coffee, Chris set the cup down and smoothed nonexistent creases from her skirt. "It's not a very interesting life," she said, choosing her words carefully. "I was born and raised, got married, had kids. My husband died a few years ago and I teach school. Sometimes I volunteer at the library. It's all excruciatingly normal."

She looked up at Evan and had a feeling he could see

right through her. But maybe that was just a guilty conscience; what she'd said was the truth, but only in the broadest sense of the word. In fact, her life had been far from normal, but that was certainly not the business of these two strangers.

She wrinkled her nose self-deprecatingly. "And I'm not very glamorous," she went on. "I tend to talk too much and clip coupons and get cranky if I forget to set the VCR for *The Young and the Restless*. Not exactly the stuff of great drama."

Evan raised an eyebrow. "Mrs. McConnell—"

"Chris," she interrupted.

"Chris. Surely you can see that there's a great story here. The story of a young widow who, one night, managed to single-handedly disarm a dangerous gunman and save the lives of at least three innocent people."

"One night"—Chris looked straight at him, grimly serious now—"I was scared out of my mind that I might die. I did whatever I had to so I wouldn't."

Her hands were trembling now, and she concentrated on bringing herself under control. "I'm lucky to have survived. It could just as easily have gone the other way," she added quietly.

"But it didn't go the other way," Evan said, realizing he was damned glad it hadn't. "You're here to tell the story."

Marla nodded enthusiastically. "A wonderful story!"

Chris closed her eyes briefly, then opened them again. "So, write a script about a woman just like me, but don't use my name. I believe it's called fiction."

"No." Marla's head shake was adamant. "It isn't the

same." The actress went on, her body taut with enthusiasm. "Do you know the kind of ratings they get for TV movies based on a true story? They're off the charts! Two and three times better than just a regular fictional story."

Evan sat back again and watched Chris's face as Marla reeled off the statistics of several recent TV films based on the sensational headlines of the day: child abuse; bravery in the face of AIDS; battered wives; a Vietnam protestor, under cover for twelve years, turning himself in. She quoted ratings shares, demographics, Emmys received. With each new number Chris's look of astonishment deepened a little more.

When Marla took a moment to breathe, Evan winked at Chris. "Impressive, isn't she?"

"What's impressive," Chris replied with a wry shake of her head, "is that anyone takes this stuff seriously."

"The networks take it very seriously," he said. "And that means the sponsors take it seriously."

Marla jumped in again. "Which means Wall Street takes it seriously. And anything that happens on Wall Street affects the whole country."

Chris stared at the actress, then sat back on the couch and crossed one leg over the other, amused skepticism scrawled across her face. "Let me see if I get what you're saying here," she said slowly. "You are sitting in my living room, drinking my coffee and eating my homemade walnut cookies, and telling me it's my patriotic duty as an American to allow you to film my life. Have I got that right?"

Marla bit her bottom lip. "If I wave the flag, will that make you say yes?"

"Nope."

Evan erupted in laughter, and Chris looked over at him, startled at first. But then her face lit up with the most open, generous, *amazing* smile—it was as though the sun had just broken through a dismal day—and she joined in his laughter. For that moment the two of them connected the way strangers at a party do when they realize they're on the same wavelength. Their smiles said that each was aware of the absurdity of the conversation, the whole situation.

Each was aware of the other.

Evan felt the smile leave his face the same moment Chris's left hers, but their gazes remained locked. Something subliminal went from her to him and back again—or was it the other way around? he wondered briefly. What had just happened had no words and needed none.

He sensed rather than saw Marla's glare of disapproval at him. "Whose side are you on anyway?" she asked.

"Marla," he said quietly, unwilling to draw his gaze away from Chris. "Wait for me in the car."

"Huh?"

"Just do it, okay?"

Puzzled, the actress stared at him, then at Chris, then back at Evan. One corner of her coral-tinted mouth turned up knowingly. "You going to use your 'persuasive powers' on Mrs. McConnell?" she purred suggestively. "Hey, if it works, I'm all for it."

She got up from the couch and adjusted her suit jacket. Then she walked to the front door and opened it wide, smiling at the sunshine.

"Looks like a couple of fans are out there," she said blithely, fluffing the curls around her neck. "I think I'll have a chat with them. I'll be waiting, Evan. And I expect results," she added, tossing the remark over her shoulder as she walked outside.

Chris shook her head, trying to overcome the dreamlike state she had fallen into when her eyes met Evan's. Now that Marla had shut the door, the room was bathed in soft shadows again. An old grandfather clock in the corner ticked loudly. Outside, several birds traded whistles and chatter.

And Evan sat across from her, watching her, his turquoise gaze piercing her with its intensity.

Lord, it was too much. Looking away, she shifted her position on the sofa cushion, pulling at her skirt so it covered her knees. Something unexpected and a little scary had just happened in this room—unless she'd imagined, even wished, the whole thing. But, no, she hadn't. The way Evan was gazing at her now made her feel exposed and way too vulnerable. She had to remember . . .

What did she have to remember? Oh, yes. The reason he was there. He wanted something from her.

"You heard Marla," Chris said briskly, hoping to shatter any leftover intimacy in the room. "The lady expects results. What happens if you don't get them?"

He didn't reply, but after a moment the taut stillness left him, and he leaned back in his chair and took a swig of his beer. "I guess I face that if and when I don't get them."

"Then you'll be facing it pretty soon. Do you work

for her? Didn't she say something about you being part-
ners?"

"It's her production company, so technically I guess I
work for her." He shrugged. "I work for anyone who can
pay my price."

"Oh."

The cynical detachment in his tone made Chris sorry
suddenly that she'd brought the conversation back to this.
She'd liked it better when his face had reflected all the
surprise, all the wonder, she knew had been on her own.

He finished off the beer, then set it down on the side
table. "Now, how about we get back to the matter at
hand? Here's the deal. Marla really wants to do this
movie, and she's willing to pay a lot of money for the
privilege."

"And I'm afraid my answer is still the same. No."

"No," he repeated. "And there's absolutely nothing I
can say to make you change your mind."

"Not a thing."

"Well, then—"

He pushed himself up from the chair and stretched.
His jacket parted with the movement of his arms and she
got a glimpse of the way his T-shirt hugged his broad
chest, and how his jeans lovingly molded his lean hips, his
muscular thighs. She swallowed down the urge to sigh
like some bewitched adolescent.

"Sorry," he said. "Late night and not much shut-eye.
I guess I should probably just say good-bye."

Good-bye? Chris blinked, taken aback by his words
and the wave of disappointment they brought. Was that
the end of it? Had it been that easy to get him to back off?

Well then, good, she told herself resolutely, rising from the couch so she could walk him to the door. He and Marla would take off now, out of town, out of her life. Yes, that was precisely what she'd wanted.

Wasn't it?

TWO

With his hand on the doorknob, Evan turned as though struck by an afterthought. "Can you recommend a good hotel?"

"Hotel?"

"Is there one here, in Loman? Or do we have to go somewhere else, maybe a bigger town?"

Chris stared at him. "Hotel?" she repeated, probably sounding feebleminded. "You're staying?"

"Sure."

She felt her mouth drop open and shut it quickly. "You haven't given up, then?"

He chuckled. "Are you kidding? Marla's never heard of the concept of gracious surrender." Leaning against the closed door, he crossed his arms over his chest and met her questioning gaze. "Let me tell you how it's going to be," he drawled. "First she'll romance you, paying lots of attention, flattering you. Then she'll set the lawyers on you with promises of money and script approval. There'll be hints about magazine articles, maybe an appearance on *Entertainment Tonight*, visits to a movie set for your children and you. All the glamour you can handle."

"Good Lord."

"If that doesn't work, she'll try to find a weak spot—your favorite charity, maybe, or a college fund—something that really means a lot to you, and she'll use that to convince you. She may even try a little gentle blackmail. She's not above it, bless her heart, if she thinks it will work. Finally, she'll bombard you with phone calls, plant items in gossip columns, get all your friends and family to nag you to death until you scream 'Yes!' at the top of your lungs, just to get her off your back."

Chris stared at him, dumbfounded. "All that?"

"Yep." Raising one eyebrow, he favored her with one of his small, cynical smiles. "Just how strong are you, Chris McConnell? Because that's the way it'll be. When Marla Simone wants something, she goes after it."

Chris felt a sinking feeling in the pit of her stomach. Saying no to Marla wasn't going to be a simple matter after all. Not to mention the fact that the actress might dig a little into Chris's past and do some damage.

Evan noticed the sudden dramatic shift in her mood, and his amusement faded. "Chris," he said. "I'm sorry."

With a jerk of her head she looked away from him, but not before he caught the alarm in her eyes. He had the urge to stroke the tension from her cheek, to take her hand in his and hold it, massaging away some of the tightness in her body.

Uh-uh, bad move. He'd met her—what? twenty minutes ago? Shared a couple of smiles and a prolonged look or two? He'd been raised in a small town and knew all about them; touching Chris would be considered too soon and way too forward for Loman, Colorado.

Evan turned and walked slowly back to the couch, where he perched on one of the arms. He reached for a cookie and took a bite. "Mrs. Fields, take a hike. These really are good, you know. And I've had the best."

"I imagine you have."

The hint of sarcasm in her tone made him glance back at her. "You're upset, aren't you?"

"Well, wouldn't you be? You've just told me that I'm about to be subjected to a siege! My life, the lives of my kids, our very existence, will never be the same. Yes, I'm good and upset!" Hands on hips, she glared at him. "And, boy, am I allergic to being manipulated."

"Me too. But that's the way the game is played."

"This is not a game. This is my life! Well, it's not going to do Marla any good, I can tell you that."

"Okay."

"In fact, it's already having the opposite effect."

"So I see."

"My mind is made up."

He held up his hands in mock surrender. "Hey, you've convinced me, I promise."

She stared at him for a moment, then her eyes narrowed. "Pardon my suspicious nature," she said slowly, her arms dropping to her sides, "but is this how it's done? Nasty Marla comes after me with both barrels blazing, and nice Evan says, 'Tsk, tsk, isn't she awful?' and then I'm so moved by your compassion that I sign on the dotted line? Good-cop bad-cop type of thing?"

He couldn't help chuckling. "I think I'm being insulted. But, no. I'm not that devious, I promise."

"Coulda fooled me," she muttered, then marched over to the coffee table and began gathering the cups and placing them on the tray.

"Chris?"

"I need to clean up here. Why don't you have another cookie? Take one to Marla out in the car. Take a bunch of them for all her fans. In fact, I'll even throw in the recipe if you'd like."

Evan leaned an elbow on the back of the couch. "But get the hell out of here, please," he said as though completing her thought.

"Something like that. There really isn't anything left to say, is there? You've come all this way for nothing."

"Have I?"

"Yes." She kept her gaze firmly fixed on the contents of the tray. "You haven't talked me into giving Marla the rights."

"Maybe not. But it wasn't for nothing, trust me."

The quiet way Evan said the words got her attention. She glanced over at him, then silently cursed herself for making a big mistake. Oh, those Aegean-tinted eyes. How could one pair of eyes convey so much?

She lifted the tray and walked toward the kitchen, not trusting herself to speak, but needing to get away from him.

He followed her. "Let me help."

"That's unnecessary. It's not heavy."

"Then I'll just accompany you. And if you don't want

to, we won't discuss Marla or the rights or anything to do with the whole project."

"Then there's not a whole lot left to talk about, is there?"

"I'll bet we could find something. If we worked at it."

"Sorry," Chris replied, determined to put an end to this, even if she was being rude. "My kids will be back soon and I have to take them shopping for shoes."

She set the tray down on the drainboard and transferred the dishes into the sink. The kitchen was small, with a round wooden table in one corner and a tiny service porch beyond that led to the backyard. One sink, two counters, one stove. Chipped white tiles and gray linoleum. Like the rest of the house, the room hadn't been modernized in twenty years. Its old-fashioned charm made up for some of the dreariness, but Chris still felt a twinge of embarrassment.

"May I dry?" Evan picked up a thin, worn terry-cloth dish towel.

"Are you sure you know how?"

"I think I can probably work it out."

He flashed her a grin, but she didn't want to respond, so she busied herself getting the soap and scouring pad from the curtained-off shelf below the sink. "Have I seen anything you've produced or written?"

"I don't know. I specialize in the can-you-top-this-dysfunction kind of TV film. And once in a while one of those small-budget, high-minded projects that no one ever sees and pays me next to nothing."

"When was the last time you worked on one of those?"

"It's been a few years. I have a certain lifestyle to support after all," he drawled sardonically. "But listen, we're not here to discuss me. About those rights—"

"You said you wouldn't bring it up again."

"I'm not trying to talk you into it, I promise. But I want to know why you're so dead set against it. Can you at least tell me that?"

Chris formulated an answer, discarded it, and formulated another. Finally, propping a hip against the edge of the counter, she turned her gaze on him. "It's not that I don't like being fussed over," she said thoughtfully, "or even that I don't feel worthy of all the fuss. I like attention as well as the next person. But what happened to me, is too . . . personal. I don't relish being invaded. Opened up for inspection. Can you understand that?"

Meeting Chris's gray eyes and hearing her simple, heartfelt words, Evan felt a little tug in the back of his throat. Ignoring his previous admonition to himself against physical contact with her, he threw the dish towel over his shoulder and took one of her hands in his. It was soft and cool, her fingers slim between his broad, blunt ones. She gave a start at the contact, but she didn't fight him.

"I do understand," he said quietly. "I don't think I'd relish being invaded either."

"Then why are you here?"

He shrugged, looking down at their joined hands and rubbing his thumb along the soft pad near her wrist. "It's a job. It's what I do."

"Invade people?"

His half-smile was rueful. "You might be amazed at

how many people love being invaded. We live in a time when the need for privacy is looked upon as abnormal."

"Yes, well, call me old-fashioned, but my privacy is real important to me."

Chris's gaze dropped to the way Evan held her fingers in his. She didn't even want to consider why she was permitting this intimacy. His skin was rougher and several shades darker than hers, and the visual contrast between his hand and hers was fascinating.

As was the stirring of her blood as his thumb moved up and down against her soft, long-untouched skin. She shivered at the shot of sheer sensation on her wrist, then up the length of her arm, branching off to the tips of her breasts, even finding its way to a private area between her thighs.

Oh, she said silently. All this from one stranger's touch. Her reaction to him, to what it told her she had been hiding from herself, was pretty frightening. She willed her body to stop trembling.

"How about we get these dishes done," she said, removing her hand from his and turning on the water.

She felt him assessing her for a moment, then he pulled the dish towel from his shoulder. "Yes, ma'am."

For a while the only sound in the room was the water gushing from the tap as Chris washed and Evan dried. When she thought she could successfully carry on a little small talk, she said casually, "Have you always wanted to be a writer?"

"Nope. I wanted to be a cowboy, then a fireman. But when I was about twelve I wrote a poem to this girl in my class who never looked at me. After she read it, she looked at me. Even let me kiss her. I decided if that was the way to get female attention, I would be a writer."

"That's downright inspiring," Chris said dryly, placing the final cup in the drainer and turning off the water. "And I suppose you have a huge house in the Hollywood Hills and go to screenings and lots of parties and wonderful restaurants?"

She bit her lip, wishing that had come out a little more flippantly. He couldn't have missed the wistfulness in her voice, and she wondered if she seemed foolish to him.

All her life, in foster home after foster home, Chris had found sorely needed escape in movie theaters and magazines filled with stories of film people. Her childhood fantasies had always revolved around her somehow being a part of the glamorous, larger-than-life world of movies. She was starstruck, that was the truth, which was why she'd allowed Marla to come to see her. She'd never had any intention of selling the actress the rights, but she hadn't been able to forfeit the chance to meet one of her childhood idols in person.

"Nope again," Evan said. "No big house. And I'm pretty solitary by nature, so I don't much care for parties. I have a place in Malibu—"

"On the ocean?"

"No, but you can see the ocean from the top of my mountain. Does that count?" he said with a small smile. "From a couple of rooms in my house, as a matter of fact. I even have a telescope so I can follow the dolphins and the whales when they migrate."

The yearning rose in her throat again and she swallowed it down. Frowning, Chris took another thin towel from a hook and dried her hands. "I've never seen the ocean."

"Really?"

Evan was startled by her statement, then added it to all the things he sensed about her already—how unexciting much of her life seemed to be. That she had high standards and wouldn't budge about selling her story. That underneath her spunk there was both tension and sadness; it was deep, almost hidden, but it called out to him like a foghorn in the mist.

He never let women get too close, never let them affect him too deeply. Keep it light and keep it temporary was his motto. But this woman got to him in a way that hadn't happened in so long, it was practically a new sensation. Something about her moved him. Right this moment he wanted to make her smile, to *give* to her.

Give to her? Make her smile? Man, oh, man. If he were smart, he'd beat it out of there pronto, dragging Marla with him. But he wasn't smart; at least not that day.

"You've really never been to the ocean?" he asked, hanging up the towel.

"Unless you count seeing *Jaws* four times."

He smiled. "Close, but not quite. Well then, if you come out to L.A., I promise a first-class tour of anything you want to see—the ocean, restaurants, Universal Studios. You name it," he finished expansively.

The softness on Chris's face was gone in an instant. Lowering her eyes, she carefully folded the dish towel and laid it on the edge of the sink. "Very good. You did that very well," she nodded.

"What?"

"Used your 'persuasive powers.' Marla will be very proud of you."

He felt like he'd been punched in the gut.

"Hey!" He grabbed her shoulders and spun her around so that she was facing him again. "That had nothing to do with Marla. Not a damned thing."

"Really?"

"Really. Nothing to do with her. I don't *want* you to sell her the rights, okay? In fact I'm damned glad you're not. For once someone is saying no to being famous."

"Then why are you dangling a trip to Los Angeles in front of me like bait? Tell me that."

The suspicion he read on her face really made him mad. He might be a lot of things—cynical and untrusting, a loner who avoided intimacy for sure—but, dammit, he was not a user, a manipulator of women.

"That was something different," he said. "That had to do with— It had to do with this!"

He brought his mouth down on hers in what began as a punishing kiss. But the moment his lips touched hers, and he heard her quick, surprised intake of breath, it changed from anger into something else, something softer, warmer.

God, she tasted good. Sweet. Hungry. Slowly, he parted her lips with his tongue, running the tip around the moist flesh just inside her mouth. He felt her own tongue answer his, tentatively at first, then with more assurance. Groaning, he pulled her closer so he could feel those firm, high breasts of hers against his chest.

"Mommy! Mommy!"

At the sound of a child's voice, Chris pulled away from Evan with a gasp. A door slammed, there was the sound of running feet, and a different child's voice shouted, "Marla Simone is sitting on a car in front of the house!"

Chris turned her back on Evan and faced the service porch just as a tiny barrel of energy jumped into her arms. Another, older child ran in and hugged her knees.

"Whoa!" Chris called out. "Watch out, you two, or you'll bowl me over!"

The little girl with her arms around Chris's neck had straight blond hair, pale skin, and chocolate surrounding her mouth that matched the brown of her huge eyes. Both she and the boy—a few years older with Chris's gray eyes—noticed Evan's presence at the same time.

The little girl stuck her thumb in her mouth while the boy said, "Who are you?"

Before Evan could answer, a shrill female voice called, "Lisa Mae, you come back here! I haven't wiped your mouth off yet."

A short, plump woman with tightly permed gray hair came bustling into the kitchen from the service porch. She seemed slightly out of breath, and when she saw Evan, she stopped short and put her hand over her heart. "Goodness. I didn't know you had company, Christine."

The little girl's face was partly buried in her mother's blouse, but she peeked out at Evan with avid curiosity. "Who is the man?" she whispered loudly.

Chris turned to Evan, the expression on her face carefully impersonal. "Evan Stone, I'd like you to meet Dora McConnell, my mother-in-law. And these are my children, Brian and Lisa McConnell. Evan is here with Ms. Simone."

"Oh, yes," Dora said with suspicion. "That actress." She shook Evan's hand quickly and dropped it. "If you're with her, why's she out there and you're in here?"

Chris cut in quickly. "Mr. Stone wanted to talk to me. He writes scripts for television," she added as though that explained everything.

The older woman eyed him with disapproval. "Does he. Hmm." Then she grabbed the dish towel, ran the edge of it under the hot water, and went to work on the chocolate stains around Lisa's mouth.

Chris took the towel from her mother-in-law. "It's all right, Mother. I'll do it."

After propping Lisa on the counter next to the sink, Chris wiped gently around her daughter's mouth. When she was done, she tweaked Lisa's nose and smiled. "Now you're gorgeous again." Kissing the child's cheek, she set her on the floor.

Evan felt a tug on his jacket pocket and looked down to see Brian staring up at him. "Do you write the scripts for *The Family Finch*?"

He hunkered down so he was at eye level with the boy. "I'm afraid not. That show is over twenty years old, a little before my time."

"I'm nine," said the little boy, "and my sister is three. How old are you?"

"Brian," Chris said. "No third degree today. Mr. Stone is just leaving."

"But he knows Marla Simone. It's *okay*, Mom."

She looked at the boy with great fondness as she

brushed back the nearly black hair that swept his fore-head. "All those reruns on the cable," she explained to Evan. "*The Partridge Family. The Brady Bunch.* But *The Family Finch* is their favorite."

"Everyone's so nice on that show," Brian said.

"It's make-believe," Dora said, "that's all."

Lisa, who was standing just behind Chris's skirt, tugged at her straight blond hair. "Marla Simone is so pretty, and I like how curly her hair is," she said.

"I'll tell her you said so," Evan said. "She'll be very pleased."

Chris nodded. "Yes, she will. Well, I'm going to walk Mr. Stone to the door. Say good-bye, kids, and then get changed to go to the mall."

Lisa hugged even closer to her mother and peeked out at him with a shy little smile. "Bye, mister."

"Good-bye, Lisa."

Evan shook Brian's hand. "See you again, Brian. Mrs. McConnell," he added, bowing his head in Dora's direction.

He followed Chris back through the small kitchen and the living room. When they got to the front door, she turned to him but avoided his eyes. Her discomfort with him was obvious. The kiss had probably been a mistake, but it had just happened, and he didn't regret it in the least.

Chris gave Evan what she hoped was a polite smile. "Now it *is* good-bye."

He shook his head slowly. "For your sake, I hope so. But I'm afraid Marla will keep upping the ante until she makes you an offer you can't refuse."

"As in *The Godfather*? I hope not."

"As in everyone has his price." Evan had assumed that same mask of detached amusement that had been her first impression of him. "As in there hasn't been a person born who can't be bought."

Her gaze roamed his face, studying his expression for clues to his behavior. "You're funny, you know."

"Ha-ha funny?"

"Complicated funny. You seem kind of cynical by nature, and then you go and do or say something sensitive. I can't make you out."

"You're probably better off not trying. Meanwhile, I'm going to do my damnedest to talk Marla out of this project."

"I appreciate it. But why?"

"Maybe because I've met someone who can't be bought and I want to reward her. Okay?"

She waved away his words. "Please, don't put me on a pedestal."

"I haven't put a woman on a pedestal in a long time. It's against my religion." He seemed to want to say something more; instead, Evan raised his hand to her face and cupped her cheek, rubbing the thumb along her jawline.

She caught her breath at the unexpectedness of his gesture, and at the quivering it sent along her nerve endings. But before she could work up a halfhearted protest, he dropped his hand to his side.

"Yeah, we'd better say good-bye," he said. "And hey, you never know, you might get lucky. It might actually *be* good-bye."

She swallowed down a feeling of desolation at his

words and nodded. "It's probably for the best, considering. . . ."

"Are you sorry?" he asked softly. "About the kiss?"

She shook her head no.

"Good. And it will never happen again."

"Why?" she blurted out without thinking, then lowered her gaze with embarrassment. "Pretend I didn't ask that. Please."

"But I'll answer it." He lifted her chin with his finger, forcing her eyes to meet his. "It's because you're fresh and clean," he said quietly, "and I haven't been either of those in years. It's because you're special and shouldn't be taken lightly, and I'm not capable of anything else. Goodbye, Chris McConnell. I'm glad we met."

Chris watched him walk out the door, watched those long legs take long strides as his boots clumped loudly on the porch steps. When he got to the sidewalk, he reached into his jacket for a box of cigarettes and shook one out. He found a book of matches in the back pocket of his jeans, his movement affording her a quick glimpse of small, tight buttocks caressed by faded denim.

He bent over to light his cigarette, blew out the match, and seemed about to flick it away, when he paused as though realizing she was still watching him. He turned around and gave her a little half-smile, held up the used match, then placed it carefully into his jacket pocket.

"No littering allowed," Evan said.

Then he nodded, turned again, and strode toward a large luxury sedan parked at the curb. Marla stood leaning against the side of the vehicle, busily signing autographs for half the town.

THREE

"Hi, Mrs. McConnell."

Chris was leaning an elbow on the counter, resting her chin in her hand and catnapping, oblivious of the sounds of the Loman Autumn Bazaar and Fair—laughter and shouting, the popping of balloons and air rifles, the tinny piping of a carousel—going on around her. The same voice repeated, "Mrs. McConnell?"

She straightened with a start, splaying her hand over her pounding heart. Bobby Charles stood at her booth with his gap-toothed grin and the cowlick that stuck up in the air like an antenna. Chris forced herself to smile.

"Hi, Bobby. Have you come for a book?"

"My mom said I had to."

"What do you like to read?"

Bobby lifted his thin shoulders in a shrug. "I don't know."

"Well, what do you read at home?"

He shrugged again. "Mostly I watch TV."

She tried not to sigh. "Don't you want to read, just a little bit, for yourself? Remember when we had story time in class?"

"Yeah, but that was in the second grade," he said with appropriate ten-year-old disgust. "We don't have story time in the fourth grade."

"What a shame. Here's a book about pirates, and I'll throw in one about a cowboy and his horse, only it takes place on another planet. How does that sound?"

"Cool."

The crackle that usually preceded loudspeaker announcements cut through the fair's background noise. A deep male voice said, "Is this thing on?" There were sounds of someone blowing into the microphone. "Am I on? I am? Okay."

Loman sheriff Jeremy Kahane always did all P.A. system announcements because it wasn't a very good system and he could yell louder than anyone else in town. After some throat-clearing, Jeremy boomed out, "Attention, attention! The raffle for the rebuilt Harley motorcycle donated by Rusty's Garage is at two o'clock in front of the bandstand. Remember, tickets are only a dollar each. Buy as many as you'd like. All proceeds go to the football field reseeding and bleacher replacement fund."

Chris handed the books to the boy, reached over to smooth down his cowlick, and watched it spring to attention again.

"Bye, Mrs. McConnell."

"Good-bye, Bobby."

Chris watched him take off into the crowd. There was a pretty good turnout this year. Most all the locals and even some people from neighboring towns had shown up. The day had started out overcast, but the late morning sun was peeking through the clouds now, and Chris suspected it would be a scorcher by late afternoon.

How she wished she could get into the spirit of the thing, but she was tired and edgy. She hadn't slept well since the night of the robbery. There were bad dreams that she couldn't remember, and any sudden sound made her jump out of her skin. She found herself trembling at the strangest times. Post-traumatic stress syndrome it was called. All her reactions were very common, and the policewoman had suggested professional help. But Chris had been through worse things in her life, and was determined to tough it out.

She straightened up. Backbone, girl, she told herself as she had many times in her life. Make an effort.

Two eight-year-old girls went by her booth, each licking an ice cream cone, each in a dress with lots of ruffles that flounced as they walked. "Hi, Mrs. McConnell," they said in unison.

"Hi, Doreen, Jennifer."

"Hi, Mrs. McConnell."

Startled at the sound of a mature male voice saying those words, Chris whipped her head around to her left.

Evan stood there, aviator sunglasses perched firmly on the bridge of his nose and a half-smile quirking up the side of his mouth, the same smile that had been invading her thoughts for the past twenty-four hours. He wore a pale green shirt, faded jeans, and the boots he'd had on the previous day. He was leaning insouciantly against the side of the booth, arms crossed over his chest.

"How long have you been there?" she asked.

"A while. You're pretty popular with kids."

"Kids are great," Chris said, then sighed. "I just wish they read a little more. I truly think there's a conspiracy to wipe out the imagination."

"So you wage your one-woman war. I guess somebody has to."

Chris gave a little shrug, and Evan thought, not for the first time, how different she was from the tinseltown women he came in contact with most of the time. She seemed so damned *real*.

She wore a white T-shirt with LOMAN SCHOOL DISTRICT stenciled on it. The shirt was tucked into an A-line cotton skirt. Her hair was pulled back off her face in a high ponytail, and there was just a touch of pink lipstick on her mouth. Except for the shadows under her eyes, she looked about eighteen.

"What do you think of our little gathering?" Chris asked him.

He gazed at the panorama around him—wooden booths and a couple of tents, kids running and screaming, parents telling them to hush. Dust. Clumps of dried grass and dead weeds. A Ferris wheel, people hawking their wares. A fair at a peaceful small town in middle America.

He hated it.

"It's definitely a gathering," he answered noncommittally, pushing himself away from his leaning post to face Chris directly. Overhead there was a hand-painted sign and he read the words aloud. "HELP SUPPORT YOUR TOWN. ONLY TEN CENTS A BOOK. LEARN ABOUT OTHER LANDS AND

OTHER PEOPLE." He lifted an eyebrow. "You expect to make a killing at ten cents a book?"

Her smile was rueful. "Every little bit helps."

"Yeah, I noticed the town is on the run-down side."

"Recession and drought'll do it every time. We do what we can to stay afloat."

He rested his elbows on the counter and grinned up at her. "You'd probably make more money if you sold kisses instead of books," he teased.

Chris's neck colored slightly. "Maybe. But then my reputation would be in tatters, and schoolteachers can't afford to have that." She turned her back to him and fussed over some of the books on the shelves behind her, straightening their spines and pushing them into groups. "I'll bring in some money later in the day," she said over her shoulder, "when it's my turn at the dunking pool."

"Dunking pool," he repeated. "I haven't seen one of those in years. When is it your turn?"

She looked at her watch. "About four."

"I think I'll stick around for that." He leaned back against one of the posts and surveyed the fair again.

"Speaking of sticking around," Chris said, "I couldn't help noticing you're still here. Can Marla be far away?"

"Not very."

"So, you found a hotel."

"A motel for me. The amazing Ms. Simone maneuvered herself some digs here in town."

"Really? I wouldn't think Marla would cotton to the Loman Arms. She doesn't seem the type to share a bathroom with twelve other people."

"No, she has her very own room and bath. The mayor put her up."

"The mayor? Frank Metzger? How did he get involved in this?"

Evan turned his head and gazed at her surprised face. "Marla paid a little call on City Hall yesterday and charmed the man. He's putty in her hands now. She's deadly, I told you that."

"You certainly did. But what does Frank have to do with—" She was interrupted by the sight of the very man they'd been discussing, bustling over to the booth with an air of self-importance.

"Chris. Got a minute?" Frank wore an awful hairpiece and, in spite of the heat, was dressed in a suit and tie. He noticed Evan and took his hand, shaking it heartily. "Mr. Stone, good to see you. Finding everything you need here in town?"

"Everything the town can provide, Frank," Evan replied, withdrawing his hand from the enthusiastic greeting.

The sound of someone blowing into the microphone was followed by an extremely loud "Is this thing on? Okay. Sarah Simms," a man boomed out. "Sarah Simms. Your dad is looking for you over at the Ferris wheel, where you were supposed to be fifteen minutes ago. Sarah Simms, your dad is looking for you."

"I just saw Sarah over at the fortune-teller booth," Frank said. "Nothing to worry about. So," he said, turning back to Chris with a broad, self-impressed smile, "what do you think of my houseguest?"

Evan's eyes narrowed as he watched Frank with Chris.

Apparently, this Metzger owned a successful insurance agency, one of the only thriving businesses in town. Thus the job of mayor. And the suit on a dusty, hot day. He was near forty and prosperous-looking, with a ring of perspiration around his hairpiece and a slight pot belly.

Evan didn't like him. He never liked hearty hand-shakers. Cornelius Conroy had been one of those—slick from the word go. He'd shake everyone's hand and slap them on the back, and then he'd do something sneaky. He'd robbed Evan's father of the farm, right out from under him.

That phony bonhomie was one of the reasons Evan hated the first part of Hollywood meetings, with the little lies about how much they loved your last project—which they probably hadn't seen—and the high hopes they had for this one—which they probably wouldn't buy. He much preferred getting right to the point, the laying of cards on the table, leaving the personalities out of it. Stabbing? Yeah, maybe. But at least not in the back.

No, Evan didn't like Frank Metzger. He also didn't like the way he was eyeing Chris.

"I hear you and Marla got along real well yesterday," Frank said, mopping his brow.

Chris lifted an eyebrow. "Is that what she told you?"

"Yes. Marla's promised to attend the dance tonight. Isn't that wonderful of her?"

"Couldn't be more wonderful."

Evan bit back a grin; he had a feeling that Frank wasn't picking up on Chris's sarcasm.

"Will you be staying for the dance?" Frank persisted. "I thought we might—"

"Sorry," she said briskly. "Lisa's getting a cold."

"Just a cold? Why don't you—"

Evan interrupted. "Listen, I'm going to walk around a bit and leave you two to your discussion. See you later."

He didn't really want to leave Chris, but he figured he'd monopolized enough of her time. Besides, there was a small curl of jealousy in the pit of his stomach at the way Frank was putting the moves on her, and he didn't want to witness any more of their interaction.

Not that Frank had a chance in hell with Chris. She didn't like the guy, and wasn't being real subtle about letting him know. But Metzger was the type who would need a battering ram in the solar plexus to hear anything he didn't want to hear.

Still, that moment of jealousy had stirred up a bunch of feelings, and Evan didn't like any of them. Man, he thought, walking along the fairground, I really don't want to be here.

There had been fairs like this one all through his childhood, and a lot of backs turned on the Stones, whispers about his mother's "carrying on." Then later, after she'd run off, gossip about his father's drinking and card playing, the general dissolution of the family. The Stone boys—he and his brother Lon—were always in fights with the other kids. Evan had been a surly, unhappy boy, no doubt about it. And in a town not unlike Loman.

He wandered over to a dusty corral and perched a boot on the wooden fence's lower railing. The October day was a hot one, and as he swiped his sleeve over his forehead, he wished he'd remembered to bring one of his Stetsons along on this trip. He watched some mediocre horseflesh being paraded around for a while. There was a decent little gelding in the corner, and the young kid holding a rope and stroking the nose of the horse had a haircut that looked as though it had been trimmed with a bowl around it—the way Evan's had all those years ago. . . .

He mentally swatted away the memory. A waste of time. Yeah, he really didn't want to be there, but Marla had dragged him along, saying it was part of their agreement. Two days, he'd promised her. Two full days. And then adios.

Marla and he had spent the previous evening arguing —he told her it would do no good to keep badgering Chris, and she told him he didn't know what he was talking about. Telling Marla no was like putting a carrot in front of a donkey. Well, let her pull whatever stunt she wanted. As of this evening, he was out of there. And good riddance. He was sorry he'd come at all.

Except for the fact that if he hadn't, he would never have met Chris McConnell. And that would have been a real shame. In fact, the thought brought a powerful, unexpected wave of sadness with it.

But Evan shook it off. The way he shook off anything he didn't want to feel. He'd had a lot of practice at that.

Chris mopped her forehead with a hanky, then fanned it in front of her face. As she'd predicted, the day had turned very hot in the past couple of hours, especially in the little booth. Frank had finally gone off, thank heaven. He'd been after her for over a year. It would be nice for the kids to have a father again. But oh, how he bored her. She wanted something more from a man, some *zest*, some *excitement*. And romance. That would be nice.

Evan, with his air of mystery and unabashed masculinity, whisked to the forefront of her mind. Frank paled so next to Evan that he became invisible. Evan was all those things her imagination craved. She told herself that it must have something to do with the fact that he was forbidden fruit, and not really interested in her. Hadn't he warned her off the day before? And kept the conversation pretty impersonal this morning? Obviously, he was just waiting until Marla gave up. That's all he'd been doing, passing the time. In Loman, poor man. What a culture shock it must be for him.

It sure had been for her seven years before. And she still had the sense she didn't really belong there. Oh, sure, as John McConnell's wife, then his widow, there'd been a certain welcome from the townspeople, but a reserved one. The kids she taught were always friendly, but their parents less so. She wasn't a local, and her past was a little vague, even mysterious. A person needed to have three generations in town, preferably in the same house, for acceptance. Seven years wasn't enough, not nearly enough.

"Mommy, Mommy."

Chris was roused from her musing with a start and turned toward the sound of Lisa's voice.

Evan was walking toward the booth, Brian on his left side, gazing up at him with near hero-worship, Lisa on the right, her small hand in his much larger one. Chris's throat ached at the picture the three of them made—the tall, sturdy man between the two most precious things in her universe.

Lisa broke away from Evan, ran around the back of the booth, and jumped into Chris's arms.

"Oof! You're getting too big for the monster attack." She gave her daughter a big kiss on the cheek. "What's up, kid?"

"Can we get both—" Lisa began to ask.

"You said we could, maybe," chimed in Brian as he ran up and placed his hands on the counter.

"Both what?"

"Cotton candy *and* popcorn," he explained.

"I see."

Evan ambled up and stood behind Brian. She could see perspiration beading his forehead and upper lip, but the effects of the day's heat didn't take away one iota from his appeal. He stood with natural grace, one hip cocked, a thumb in the loop of his jeans. If there had ever been a real-life man—as opposed to a movie star—who radiated understated but deadly sensuality like this one did, she honestly couldn't remember. She could feel her body tightening in reaction to him, and she wished she'd worn something other than a thin T-shirt.

"How did you get into the act?" she asked him, making sure Lisa was shielding her breasts.

"I ran into these two over by the horses. They were having a little set-to."

"He was pulling my hair, Mommy," Lisa said in her sweet little martyr voice.

"Well, she was pinching me!"

"Hush, both of you," Chris said. "It's too hot to

fight." She looked from Brian to Lisa. "Did you eat your lunch?"

"I had two hot dogs," her son said.

"And I had one," Lisa said. "Even the bun."

"Well, then I think we can make an exception to the rule today."

"Yes!" Brian said. "I sure hope Lisa doesn't barf." Chortling with laughter, he peered up at Evan. "She does that sometimes, all these yucky little pieces of goop—"

"Mommy, make him stop." Lisa hid her head in Chris's neck.

"Come on, Brian," Chris admonished. "You've had your share of upset stomachs yourself."

She set Lisa down and the little girl scurried out from behind the counter and stuck her tongue out at her brother. Chris reached for her purse. "Lisa, cut it out. So, how much do we need?"

"Let me," Evan said, taking some bills from his pocket. Chris opened her mouth to protest, but he waved her objections away. "I want to. Now," he said, turning to Brian, "how much?"

"Two dollars will more than do it," Chris said. When Evan counted out four bills, she added, "That's two total."

Evan hunkered down so he was on eye level with the children. It amazed her how he dropped his don't-get-close persona when he talked to her kids. "Listen," he said. "I want your promise that you will use only one dollar each for food. Spend the rest on games or toys, okay? Maybe you can even buy a couple of books from your mother."

Brian gave him a look of disbelief. "Are you kidding? We got a whole bunch of books. Have you seen my mom's bedroom?"

One side of Evan's mouth twitched. "No, I haven't."

"Well, she has bookshelves up to here." He raised one thin arm as high over his head as he could, making his T-shirt hike up past his belly button.

"Up to here," Lisa echoed, raising her own arm in imitation of her brother.

"And movies too. Sometimes you can't find anything because of all the books and tapes!"

"That'll just about do it, you two," Chris interjected. "Run along. Brian, you look out for your sister. I'll catch up with both of you later."

She gazed fondly after them as they walked away, the big brother—whose recent growth spurt had rendered his arms and legs even skinnier than before—reluctantly taking the hand of his much smaller, much daintier younger sister.

Evan's voice was husky with some mysterious emotion as he said, "I think you like your kids, Mrs. McConnell."

She tore her gaze away from her children and found herself staring into a pair of magical turquoise eyes. He'd removed his sunglasses, and she swallowed before she was able to reply. "Having them was the best thing I've ever done. Do you have children?"

He furrowed his brows and put the sunglasses back on. "No," he said abruptly. "I've never wanted any."

Why? she wanted to ask, but it was none of her business. She looked away again, in the direction her children had gone. "I wish they weren't growing up so fast.

They're both still at that stage of, I don't know, innocence. Before the world gets to them."

Out of the corner of her eye she could see him nodding. "Yeah," he said. "When did the world get to you?"

"When I was way too young."

"Yeah," he said again as though he knew just what she was saying, and she thought he probably did. If she'd learned anything about human nature, it was that you didn't get that bone-deep cynical coming from a happy, well-adjusted childhood.

"Is this thing on? Okay. Ladies and gentlemen! It's time for the auction and raffle for the Harley. And have we got a surprise for you. In a few minutes we'll be welcoming an extra-special auctioneer! Miss Marla Simone!"

The whole fair reacted to the news. Applause, whistles, surprised chatter. As though someone had tipped the earth, everyone moved from all corners of the fairground and converged on the bandstand area.

Chris found the kids and Dora toward the back of the crowd, seated on a bench in the shade. Lisa had her thumb in her mouth and was leaning against her grandmother's ample arm. Brian was complaining bitterly, because he wanted to be up toward the front with his friends. Dora thought Brian should stay with them, but Chris—with as much patience as she could muster—overruled her and gave him permission to take off.

All those years ago, after Chris had met John McConnell in Boulder, he used to tell her amusing stories of his mother's overprotectiveness, and she would insist that he had to be exaggerating. But he hadn't been. If it were up to Dora, both Brian and Lisa would be wrapped in cotton and sequestered till they left for college.

The crowd buzzed with excitement, everyone in town straining for a glimpse of Marla. Chris couldn't see anything but a sea of backs, which was fine with her; she'd had plenty of glimpses of Marla the day before, thank you. She didn't need to see her ever again.

Chris plopped herself down on the wooden bench next to her mother-in-law and leaned back against the trunk of the tree behind it. Between the lack of sleep and standing on her feet all morning, she was bone weary. In spite of the crowd in front, it was peaceful in the shade.

She heard old Mr. Dobson taking bids on a "nearly new" divan, a cherished family desk, a year's supply of vitamins, and two free appointments for a cut and perm at Hair by Carrie. She let the sounds of the auction wash over her until she was in a half-awake, half-asleep state.

Evan and she were together, walking along a white, sandy beach at sunset, her hair unbound and no shoes on her feet, their hands entwined. A salt-smelling breeze, soft waves, a sky of incredible blue, and the heat from the sun just warm enough but not too warm. He turned to her, his eyes the very same color as the ocean, and smiled tenderly. . . .

"Ladies and gentlemen!"

Chris was jolted awake by Jeremy Kahane's bombastic announcement.

"Please welcome the star of *The Family Finch* and numerous other television shows—Miss Marla Simone!"

There were loud whistles and cheers from the crowd,

then Marla's sexy whisper came over the loudspeaker. "Thank you so much." More applause and whistles. "Thank you, you're all so sweet, thank you. I really appreciate your gracious welcome. But there is a reason I'm here, so please, everyone join me in thanking the *real* star of the day, Chris McConnell!"

Chris sat up with a start as several of the townsfolk looked back at her and, to the sound of more applause, beamed their approval. There was not much she could do but smile weakly and wave.

She assumed that was the end of what was required of her, but she should have known better. Marla wasn't through with her yet.

"I'm here in your lovely town at Chris's invitation," the actress purred, all gracious generosity. "I'm trying to convince her to let me portray her on television, to tell her story, her *brave* story, to the American public. We have so few role models today, I think the time is ripe to honor a real American hero!"

There were more cheers and whistles, more looks sent Chris's way. She wanted to disappear. How dare she! How dare Marla get everyone else in the town involved like this!

"Chris," Marla said. "Come on up and take a bow!"

Chris stayed put, crossing her arms over her chest. "No thanks!" she called out with as much good humor as she could muster. "I'm too hot and too tired!"

"Everyone? Let's give Chris some encouragement!"

Marla led the applause, which grew and grew till Chris was hustled out of her seat and pulled toward the bandstand by a few of her students. She found herself lifted onto the stage right next to Marla. The actress was dressed in a pink, halter-topped sundress that molded her full breasts and tiny waist perfectly. Her hair was all shiny, bouncy curls and her makeup perfect.

Standing next to the actress, Chris felt hot and sweaty and completely unglamorous in her plain T-shirt and skirt. Smiling warmly, Marla grabbed her hand and held it up in the air as if Chris were a champion boxer. She had to tamp down the urge to place her hands around the diminutive woman's throat and squeeze the life out of her. Instead, Chris smiled and yanked her hand free. Waving, she backed away with the aim of getting off the stage as quickly as possible.

Marla spoke into the mike. "Are you gonna let me play you on TV, Chris?" she asked sweetly. "Everybody out there really wants you to, don't you, everybody?"

The crowd stomped and clapped and whistled again. Chris shouted out, "Sorry, but no thanks!"

She waved graciously, slanted an I'll-get-you-for-this look at Marla, and headed for the stairs on the side of the platform. Several well-wishers waited for her there, and her heart started thumping; she felt more alarm than anger now.

She looked around her for a way to escape. Marla was to her right, the steps were full of her admirers. Feeling a little like a trapped animal, she darted to the front of the stage; more people surged toward her, laughing, applauding, their arms reaching up. She fought down the urge to scream, but could feel the panic starting to take her over.

"Chris! Over here!"

She turned in the direction of the voice. Without thinking she ran blindly toward it, to the front corner of the stage, closed her eyes, and lunged forward.

Right into Evan's arms.

FOUR

"Oh!" Chris said.

"Oh, yourself," Evan said with a grim smile, one arm cradling her shoulders, the other under her knees.

"What are you doing here?"

"I thought you might need some rescuing." As he moved away from the bandstand and toward a nearby grove of trees, he added, "This is easier if you put your arms around my neck."

Chris looked past his shoulder, then at him. "I think a better idea would be if you put me down."

"In a minute."

Behind him, Evan heard Marla purring something to the audience, and he found himself getting angry with her again. He'd watched the whole thing from the sidelines—the urging, the wheedling, the manipulating. He'd even tuned in to Chris's incipient panic attack, almost experiencing it with her. In spite of his advice to himself to stay out of things, he'd found himself working his way to the bandstand and happened to be perfectly positioned so that Chris could jump into his outstretched arms.

The rescuer, he thought sardonically. Pretty funny. He'd never been able to save anyone from anything.

He carried her around to the rear of the bandstand and several yards farther on, to a grove of tall old aspens. Enough of them still had their leaves, brown and yellow as they were, so that there was some shade from the sun, even a slight breeze. He could still hear Marla's voice as she led the raffle for the Harley, but it was more in the background now.

Chris was still in his arms, looking up at him with a tense, quizzical expression on her face. "Now will you put me down?"

"Nope. I'm not quite ready yet." He leaned back against a gnarled trunk and adjusted their positions so she was more firmly in his arms. They were also now hidden from craning necks and prying eyes trying to peer at them through the trees.

"Well then, I guess I should say thank you for catching me like that."

His mouth quirked up. "I sense a little reluctance in that line reading."

"That's because I—well, I mean, how'd you come to be there?"

He shrugged. "I woke up this morning and thought to myself, sometime today I'm going to catch me a woman. And suddenly there you were."

"Glad I could oblige. And you really do need to put me down."

He didn't want to. She was gazing up at him with a

shy wariness that was appealing. Some of her hair had come undone from her ponytail and lay around her face in pale, nearly white tendrils, curling softly in the heat of the day. He noticed the fullness of her mouth, the faint line of perspiration above the upper lip, the hint of pink lipstick applied earlier in the morning and mostly rubbed off now. The tip of her tongue darted out and licked her lips quickly, as though they had suddenly gone dry, and Evan felt a sharp surge of arousal that hadn't been there just a moment earlier.

"Uh, Evan?" she said quietly, that soft, honeyed rasp in her voice sounding more erotic than he imagined she was aware of. "You really need to put me down."

Man, he didn't want to.

But he did.

Chris brushed off the back of her skirt, avoiding his eyes. "That woman is something else, isn't she?"

"Woman?"

"Marla Simone. Fondly referred to as Killer by her close friends. And to think I used to admire her. Tonight I'm going home and destroying my Marla Simone Fan Club card."

"I'm sorry she embarrassed you."

"Not just embarrassed. She got me pretty riled up too." Placing her hands on her hips, Chris glared at him. "Why won't she let no be no?"

"Marla's used to a whole other way of dealing with people than you are, Chris. It's not personal. She's playing by her rules, you're playing by yours."

He reached over and stroked along her cheek with his thumb. Startled, she jumped back as though he'd scorched her. Her nerves seemed to be strung tighter than a drum.

He crossed his arms over his chest, his hands under his armpits, so he wouldn't be tempted to touch her again. "You going to be okay?" he asked.

"What I'm going to be is ruined in this town. You did just carry me off into the woods, you know—the macho Hollywood writer and the schoolmarm." She reached up and yanked at her hair with both hands, pulling her ponytail tighter to her head. "I'd better get myself back out there before they make us the hot topic at church tomorrow."

She gave the rubber band one final snap, then wiped across her forehead with the back of her hand.

"Is what others think of you so important?" Evan asked.

With her head cocked to one side, she looked at him. "Hey, mister, this is a small town. Do you have any experience with small towns?"

"As a matter of fact, I was born and raised in one."

"Then you'll understand. I have children and a job teaching children. I need to be squeaky clean. Which does not include being hefted into the arms of a veritable stranger and spirited off for parts unknown."

"You're right. Sorry. Not for the act, but for the ramifications." He shrugged his shoulders. "I just like spending time with you, that's all."

She stared at him for a moment, a small furrow between her eyebrows. "Yeah, well, the feeling is mutual, to tell the truth. But where does that get us?"

With that pronouncement, Chris turned and took off

in the direction of the bandstand. He didn't follow. Instead, he took note of the determination in her stride, the tension in her shoulders and clenched fists, and the subtle sway of her hips under her skirt. The way her hair, now firmly disciplined again, swished back and forth as she put more and more distance between them.

He wanted to call her back. But he didn't. Where *would* it get them?

"Whoooops!" *Splash!*

Laughing along with the crowd, Chris dragged her hair out of her eyes as she stood up in the dunking pool. "I'll get you for that, Charlie Simms," she shouted. "Just see if I don't!"

"My turn, my turn!" cried one of the other children.

"I think not," Chris said, letting herself be helped out of the water by the school principal. "I'm halfway to drowning as it is."

She shivered a little, and looked up gratefully as he draped a large towel over her shoulders and handed her another for her hair. She pulled the rubber band off and shook her head. That felt good. She'd been wanting to let her hair down, in more ways than one, all day. The next victim was perched on the stool under the target, and about thirty or so people were watching.

As she sat on a chair, rubbing the towel into her hair, Chris let her gaze wander over the assembled crowd. No Evan. He'd said he'd watch her stint at the dunking pool, but he'd probably exited the whole corny scene a while ago.

She played back their earlier conversation and shook her head. How could she? Lecturing him about small-town gossip. How provincial she must have sounded.

And it had been only a half-truth, a cover-up for what she'd really wanted to say. *Thank you for rescuing me.*

She'd been terrified up there on the bandstand. What she'd really wanted to do with Evan, instead of spouting garbage about squeaky-clean reputations, was to jump right back into his arms, back to that feeling she'd had as he carried her away from the bandstand, the feeling that she could ease up, finally, stop holding it all in. That she'd come to a strong, safe harbor for the first time in her life.

Why in the world she'd bestowed that trust on Evan, she had no idea. But it wasn't only a safe harbor that he represented. Oh, no. He set her whole being to tingling in an aroused, sensual way that she had never experienced before. Even now, at the thought of him, she could feel her body responding in a strange and wonderful way that wouldn't do at all. Not while sitting in full view of most of the town.

Put it away, she told herself sternly, put away the stray thoughts about Evan, they do you no good at all. It was amazing how much room he'd taken up in her head for the past twenty-four hours. It was time to take herself firmly in hand, to banish the fantasy and get back to reality. It was time to put away, also, all the disturbing thoughts about the night of the robbery. It was over. *Over.*

She'd scoop up the kids and take them home. Get back to her life, her real life.

"Why, Evan Stone, as I live and breathe."

He didn't bother to turn around. "What do you want Marla?"

"Why are you skulking like this, hidden away behind this . . . ? Oh, I see."

In the distance, Chris handed a couple of towels to someone, smiling her thanks.

"So," Marla said, "that's what we're up to. We're taking peeks at Chris as she gets herself dunked, are we? Checking her out as if she were a contestant in a wet T-shirt contest?"

Evan counted to ten before he turned around to face Marla. He'd learned long ago not to let others see they were getting to him. It gave them too much power. And Marla loved having power over others.

Besides, she was right. He'd kept himself out of sight behind a booth because he'd been staring at Chris, at the way her damp T-shirt clung to her and the way her nipples beaded from the cold. He was being voyeuristic; his disgust with himself only added to his irritation with Marla.

He allowed himself one final look at Chris as she waved at someone nearby, then took off in the direction of the carousel. Turning to Marla, Evan draped his arms across his chest and regarded her.

"You've been pretty busy yourself." He kept his tone cool. "But from what I can tell, it hasn't done much good. The lady turned you down. Again. And in public."

Marla slid her perfectly manicured hand up his arm,

then down again, stroking him the way she always did. He wanted to flick her hand off like a pesky mosquito, but he stood there and took it.

"Silly Evan," she cooed. "It's only a matter of time, you know that."

"Really?"

"Of course. I'll find a way to get her to change her mind." Her nails scratched lightly over his biceps.

He clamped a hand over hers. "Cut it out."

"What's the matter? Ticklish?"

"More like allergic."

With that little cat smile of hers, Marla eased her body closer till it was touching his. Yanking her hand out from under his, she transferred it to his chest, her fingernails raking through the thatch of hair exposed by the open neck of his shirt. "Come on, Evan, tell me you don't find me interesting."

"You're interesting all right. Fascinating, even. And transparent too. What do you want, Marla?"

"You."

"Bull," he said softly. "You want Chris to sell you the rights, and you think I can help, but I can't. I already told you. So knock it off."

Marla stayed glued to him, her head tilted way back so she could gaze at him through her thick lashes. Then her eyes opened wide and she grinned. "Oh, my. Evan! I just got it. You like her, don't you? I mean, *really* like her."

"Cut it out, Marla." His jaw was clenched now and he wanted to grab her hand again, this time squeezing it till she cried out.

Her laugh was a merry, phony tinkle. "Dear me," she

said, one index finger over her mouth in mock surprise, "could it be that the famous Evan Stone, the man who never lets anyone or anything get close to him, has fallen for a little nobody from a nowhere town? Fallen for the Widow McConnell?"

He grabbed her hand and pushed it away from his chest. "I said cut it out."

Chris rounded the corner near the arts and crafts tent and pulled up short. Evan and Marla were fifty feet away, talking in what seemed to be intimate terms. Marla was stroking his arm, then his chest, moving closer and closer to him. And he didn't seem in any hurry to stop her.

Of course, she thought. Of course. Marla and Evan were traveling together, and were probably sharing a bed too. Maybe it was a casual, occasional thing, the way they conducted affairs in Hollywood, but it was there. Her body language with him—yesterday at the house, and to-day for sure—was familiar, and certainly provocative.

If Chris had felt dislike for Marla before, now she could add a new dimension to that dislike. Envy, pure and simple . . . and deadly. Damn the woman.

Her stomach churned with emotion. Dear Lord, she thought, what was she doing? Yearning for what she couldn't have, lusting after an unavailable man, wanting him with a fierceness that was staggering in its intensity, feeling more resentment toward another woman than she thought possible.

Where was all this *passion* coming from? She'd buried that wild, volatile part of herself years before, dug a hole and pounded the earth in after it, so that it could never resurface again. But somehow, since the night of the robbery—no, since the first moment she'd set eyes on Evan —it had escaped, erupting like a volcano.

Covering her mouth with her hand, Chris ran toward the old boathouse, which was merely a deck of dried, rotting planks and a small enclosed area lined with benches, used mostly by kids on summer nights. She scurried to a bench and sat down, staring off into the distance. But she didn't really see anything. Her mind was spinning, spinning out of control.

Out of the corner of his eye Evan noticed a flash of white. It was Chris, taking off like a bat out of hell. Something was wrong, he knew it. He wanted to, needed to, run after her, but not with Marla looking on.

He forced himself to relax out of his defensive posture. "Look, Marla," he said easily. "You're half right. I do like the woman, but not the way you think I do. She reminds me of someone I used to know, that's all. I feel kind of . . . protective toward her. Weird, huh. Look, I'm going back to town now," he went on. "Let's meet up again for dinner, okay? About seven?"

Marla regarded him with suspicion for a moment, then shrugged. "All right."

He waited while she walked away from him. A couple of eager fans caught up to her, and she did her gracious "What? Little old me?" bit with them. Keeping a deliberately casual pace, Evan strolled off in the direction he'd seen Chris go, gazing up at the sky. The sun was setting now, taking with it the warmth of an Indian summer day. After her repeated dunkings, Chris would be getting chilled.

When he was out of Marla's sight, Evan broke into a run. Where had Chris gone? He couldn't shake off a sense of urgency about finding her. After passing through the grove, he came to a deserted-looking boathouse, filled with shadows from the day's end. He sped across the dock area, his feet making a loud pounding noise on the loose wooden slats.

"Chris?" he called out. "Chris, where are you?"

Oh, God, Chris thought as the sound of the footsteps registered in her brain. The same sound as . . .

Oh, God! My children!

Gut-stabbing panic invaded every part of her and she stood, her hand over her mouth to hold back a scream, looking around her wildly for a place to escape. But there was only the wall of the boathouse on one side and the pounding, pounding, pounding on the other.

Evan found her huddled in a corner near a dusty window, wild-eyed, her hair flowing around her shoulders. She was shaking, her arms wrapped around her rib cage as though she were trying to hold herself together.

"Chris."

She held her hands up in front of her like a shield. "No! Stay away!"

"Chris, it's me, Evan."

He saw his name register, and then she frowned in puzzlement. Moving a little closer to her, he touched her arm gently. She stared at his hand as though she didn't understand the gesture, then raised her gaze to him. Her gray eyes were wide with horror.

"Evan. I was so s-s-scared."

He gripped her arm harder and moved her over to a nearby bench. Sitting, he pulled her down next to him. He couldn't believe how much she was trembling. Easing her head onto his shoulder, he held her tightly, murmuring, "Shh, quiet now. It's okay."

"So scared." Her voice was muffled by his neck.

"I didn't mean to scare you. What was it that I did?"

"Footsteps. That pounding behind me just now. That's the way it was that night."

"What night? Oh, I see."

Memories came at Chris one after the other at high speed, bombarding her head with pictures, like a nightmarish arcade game. Terrifying pictures, terrifying memories.

"I could hear him before I saw him," she said, taking a quick, panicked breath. "He ran up right behind me and put the gun to my head. I could feel the barrel pressing against my temple and I froze. I was so terrified."

"Of course you were."

In some distant part of her brain she was aware of Evan stroking her hair, but it barely registered. "I thought I was going to die," she went on. "And then I thought, my God, my children will be orphans. What would happen to them? I couldn't stop shaking. He was shaking too. . . ." She would never forget the cold steel of the gun's barrel jiggling against her temple, the sense of helplessness, the stark horror of the moment. "And I remember thinking, what if the gun goes off accidentally? How unfair that would be. . . ."

"Yes," he soothed. "Yes."

"And then I thought, no, no, no. I am not going to die like this. I mean, if I can help it, I'm not going to die. And I made myself take deep breaths and count slowly." She took in huge gulps of oxygen as she spoke, unconsciously mimicking the way she'd reacted that night. "It was so hard to make myself stop shaking, but I had to, do you see?"

Chris's hair was damp and smelled of chlorine. Evan stroked it slowly, gently, pulling her even more tightly against him to warm her. But she jerked her body away from his, and stared at him and through him at the same time. "Do you see?"

"Yes, I see."

He realized that Chris was not only reliving the night of the robbery, but that she probably hadn't talked about it *since* that night. Good Lord, he thought, hadn't she had any help coping with the aftermath? Apparently not. No, she'd been holding it all in, not unburdening herself to anyone, and now it was all coming out in a great, relieved rush. Thank God, he thought with silent gratitude. Thank God he could be there for her.

He took her hands between his and tried to rub the chill out of them. "Tell me, Chris, tell me all of it."

She swallowed, and he could see her trying to focus her gaze on him, but she was still back there, still caught up in the terror of that night. "When I could speak without shaking, I said, listen, I think we need to talk about this. And he made the gun click, you know, like the safety was off or he was cocking it—I don't know what, I don't know about guns. . . ."

"Go on."

"And I knew that now I was in real danger, and I said, look, you can trust me. I'm not going to move, I promise. Just talk to me a little, please. He was breathing so hard and I said, I'm going to turn now and face you, okay? I want to talk to you. And I turned, real slowly, and the only thing I could see was his eyes. He was wearing a mask, it was a kid's Halloween thing, some monster mask —green and black with painted red teardrops. Like blood. Creepy."

She shivered again, and Evan squeezed her hands comfortingly.

"But I could see his eyes behind the mask," Chris went on with eyes closed, rocking her body back and forth, her hands twisting around each other. "They were wide and staring, and the pupils were enormous, and I knew he was on something. I kept my voice real calm—it was the hardest thing I've ever done. I wanted to scream at him and claw his face, but he had this gun . . ."

"Yes."

"So I talked, you know, really soothingly." Chris opened her eyes and met Evan's gaze. "I do that, some-times, when one of the kids is sick, I read to them and talk to them quietly. It's almost . . . hypnotic, you know what I mean?"

"Yes."

"After a while I could see him relaxing, just slightly.

Both of us. Calmer." Her rocking movement slackened as she told this part; again her body was recreating the night along with her mind.

"And then I remembered," she went on, "a long time ago, in Chicago, when I was just a kid on the streets, I don't know, fifteen or so, this guy showed me how to defend myself." She focused on a point over Evan's shoulder, recalling other difficult, frightening times spent alone. Always alone. Forever, it seemed.

"Chris?" Evan said.

She heard him and shook her head to clear it. "It wasn't karate or anything like that. Just two fingers in the eyes, or a knee to the groin, or a quick whack on the wrist, whichever was most available. And I kept talking and talking to the kid, and I could see him letting his guard down, and then, wham! I got him." She made a sharp chopping gesture with her hand to demonstrate. "He never saw my fist coming up, and I smashed it into his wrist. I think I broke it—you know, that superhuman energy you read about, like a mother lifting a car to rescue her baby, that kind?"

"Yes."

"And the gun went flying and the kid was so startled, by the time he even thought about retrieving it, the cops were there. And then I started shaking again."

Even though the bad part of Chris's story was over, her trembling increased. Evan pulled her tightly against his chest, wanting to give her all the support his arms could offer. "So brave," he murmured against her hair. "So very brave."

He could feel her head moving from side to side

against his shoulder. "No, not brave. Scared. What if it hadn't worked? What if he'd killed me and all the others too? That poor, sick woman that he'd tied up—she was a diabetic and she was having some kind of reaction. She was quaking from the terror, crying and moaning the whole time. What if he'd killed us all?"

"He might have . . . if you hadn't been there; if you hadn't done what you did. Shh, now. Shh."

Chris heard Evan's words, felt his broad hand massaging up and down her back, then over her hair, smoothing it in firm, sure strokes. She didn't know how long she stayed where she was, only that eventually her heartbeats began to slow down and her breathing became a little easier. And slowly she returned to the present. The nightmare she had just revisited began to fade into a series of distorted images and emotions with less and less power to terrorize her.

She let out a huge, shuddering sigh. Oh, how good, how *necessary*, it had felt to talk about that night, to purge herself of the horror. And how safe it felt to be enveloped in Evan's arms. They were so strong, so capable of containing all her fears. Why, she wondered again, did she feel so secure? He was practically a stranger. But she felt as though she could remain just as she was forever. The steady strokes of his broad hand over her head felt like a balm, a tranquilizer. She could almost fall asleep.

"Chris?"

"Hmm."

"How are you doing?"

"Better now. Thank you."

"No need."

Her mind was filled with cobwebs, and her head felt as if it weighed a hundred pounds, but she raised it and gazed at Evan. "I mean it," she said softly; it was an effort to form the words. "Thank you. I've been holding that in for days and days, and didn't even know it."

"Yeah."

Those startling eyes of his were less intense as he gazed at her; softer, somehow, filled with empathy. He raised his hand and cupped her cheek. She let her head fall to the side and rest against his hand.

"Why haven't you talked about it?" he asked quietly. "Don't you have a close friend, someone from your family?"

"I don't have a family. Never have." Her eyelids felt so heavy. She knew she'd just said something she didn't want to say, but in her exhaustion her barriers were lowered. "I don't have anyone to talk to."

He stroked his thumb along the ridge of her cheekbone. "A loner, just like me."

Loner. Evan . . . alone? A scene came floating into Chris's head then, of Marla and Evan together, their bodies touching. That was what she'd been trying to remember, why she'd run away from the fair.

Frowning, she lifted her head from the cradle of Evan's hand and glared at him. "You and Marla."

"What about me and Marla?"

"You're . . ." She shook her head. "Forget it."

"We're what?"

"Lovers," she blurted out.

"No, we're not."

"Not?"

"Not."

"Why not?"

"I'm not interested."

"She is."

"When it suits her." One side of his mouth quirked up. "I make it a habit not to get involved with actresses. Too many egos around the breakfast table. My own included."

She liked his answer; he was telling the truth, no doubt about it. Yes, she liked his answer very much.

"I'm so tired." She stifled a yawn and once more rested her head against his shoulder. His arms folded around her, and she liked that very much too. "So tired."

She could hear his chest rumbling as he chuckled. "Feel free to conk out on me anytime you'd like."

"Can't," she murmured against the soft cotton of his shirt. "Have to get back."

"Chris?"

He nuzzled the skin below her ear. It felt awfully good. "Hmm?"

"Why don't you have a close friend? Or a family?"

She moved her head from side to side, allowing him easier access to her neck. "No questions, Evan. Please."

"All right. No questions."

Something in the husky tone of his voice made her raise her head and look at him. From the way his nostrils flared slightly and his gaze dipped to her mouth, she knew he was about to kiss her. She was much too tired to stop him.

And didn't want to.

FIVE

She closed her eyes and felt the warmth of his breath right before the moment of contact. She sighed. How soft his mouth was against hers. At first. Soft and seeking, his lips rubbing gently back and forth over hers. The tip of his tongue slid along her upper lip, then the lower, and she parted them for him, welcoming him inside.

And then it wasn't gentle anymore. Then there was a fierce, urgent hunger from both of them.

"Yes, yes," he said, then plunged his tongue into her mouth, seeking, caressing, every bit of skin she could give him. And she wanted to give him all of it; her tongue met his with equal fervor and suddenly the exhaustion was gone. Every part of her body responded to Evan as though summoned to attention. Her skin tingled with awareness, and she could feel the tips of her breasts harden with desire, the muscles buried deep in her womb clench with instant burning need.

All that had happened before, her reliving of that

night, her drowsiness, even the envy and resentment of Marla, evaporated in the heat that Evan's mouth brought to the very core of her being. She was being swept away, and rode the tide of arousal and passion with abandon.

"Chris," he said, breaking the kiss and murmuring in her ear. His tongue circled the whorls and crevices there with excruciating thoroughness. "You taste so good."

"Oh, Evan," she sighed, squirming from his onslaught, wanting his hands all over her, everywhere.

"You're so real, so sweet," he whispered. "I didn't know they made women like you anymore."

An alarm went off in the back of Chris's brain.

"So good," Evan said, licking the side of her neck.

What was he saying?

"So genuine," he went on. "Not a fake bone in your body. And your body. I can't get enough of it, of you."

Somewhere in her befogged state of mind his words registered and she wrenched herself out of his embrace. "No," she said, staring at Evan and shaking her head. "No," she repeated. "No."

Then she rose from the bench and ran out of the boathouse. He followed and caught up to her at the edge of the dock. Grabbing her elbow, he turned her to face him.

"What's the matter?" he said, holding both her arms. "What's going on?"

"I'm not all those things," she cried out. "I'm not real or genuine or even very good. If you knew me, you wouldn't say that."

"What the hell are you talking about?"

"My life is a lie! I—" Horrified at what she wanted to

say to Evan, at what she'd almost let slip, Chris put both hands over her mouth for a moment and shook her head. "Go away. Please, go away!"

"Go away?" he repeated, not sure he'd heard her correctly.

"Yes."

Evan stared at Chris. What the hell was going on here? He'd held her and soothed her, and listened to her when she had so desperately needed it. And then, out of nowhere, this sudden mood shift, this putting a halt to the most incredible sexual attraction. Out of nowhere he was being treated like a leper. Why?

He was angry. And perplexed. And most of all, hurt. The flicker of interest, of hope, he'd allowed himself with this woman had obviously been a major mistake.

But Evan Stone never stayed where he wasn't wanted. "Fine," he said sharply. "I'm out of here."

Chris turned her back to him and wrapped her arms around her midriff again. Her shoulders were hunched with tension while the sun's last rays picked up white-gold wisps of her hair and made them glow.

Evan took off, breaking into a run, desperate in his hurt and anger to be away from her.

"Dammit, Marla," Evan said, "I'm not going in there. Got that? You want to give it one more try, be my guest. Make a damn fool of yourself if you want to. I will be sitting in this car, at this steering wheel—"

"Hey, slow down," Marla said not for the first time.

"—smoking a cigarette," he went on as though she

hadn't said a word. "It should take me about seven minutes. You have exactly that much time to get back into this car, because when I put the cigarette out, I'm taking off. To the airport, to the friendly skies, back to L.A."

Evan took the turn onto Chris's street as though he were racing in the Indy 500, then reduced his speed, on the lookout for children playing in the road. There were none. "Away from all of this," he said, sweeping his arm in a gesture that took in the modest homes and sidewalks visible from the window. "If you're not back here in seven minutes, you can thumb it to Denver. You probably won't have any trouble getting a ride. Hell, the mayor'll probably carry you all the way."

He pulled up in front of Chris's house, slammed on the brake, and turned off the engine, leaving the battery on. He punched the electric window button and watched the glass lower while reaching with his other hand into his pocket for a cigarette. "Dammit," he said, smacking the steering wheel. "I forgot to buy some. Okay, you got seven minutes anyway. Clock's running."

Marla stared at him with a look that could be described only as trepidation. Evan had never seen her cowed before, but then Ms. Simone had never seen his temper, had she? When provoked, it was fairly awesome. It had gotten him in trouble more than once, and it was boiling up at the moment.

Frowning, Marla reached for the door handle, then glanced back at him. "I'll be back soon."

"See to it," he barked.

After the door closed, he slumped down in his seat. His lids felt too damned heavy and he leaned back against the headrest and cursed softly. The hammering behind his eyes was almost rhythmical in its intensity, and he wished to hell it would stop.

He hadn't drunk himself into a stupor over a woman in years, but the night before that was just what he'd done. He'd cancelled dinner with Marla, bought himself a bottle, locked his motel room door, and drunk himself good and unconscious . . . over Chris. That morning he had a head the size of Alaska, his tongue was covered with enough fuzz for a sheep-shearing contest, and he was in a piss-poor mood. Even the original never-give-up kid, Marla Simone, was afraid of him. Good, she deserved it; if it hadn't been for her lame idea about filming Chris's story, he would never have met the woman, would never have aroused all these stupid emotions.

What had he said yesterday that had made Chris turn on him so suddenly? Hell, he not only couldn't remember what he'd said, he couldn't remember talking. Only burning up with urgency, a fever to connect with her out there at the boathouse, a fever that had gone past reason or memory.

Then she'd shut down and told him to take a hike, in no uncertain terms.

Fine. That's just what he would do. As soon as Marla got the door slammed in her face one more time, they were out of there. And not a moment too soon.

"Hi, Mr. Stone."

Scowling, Evan opened one eye and angled his head to his left. Brian and a couple of his friends stood by the driver's door, peering in the open window. Brian was grinning from ear to ear. "Wouldja look at all those knobs and buttons and things," he said to his buddies, then turned back to Evan. "How fast does it go?"

Evan shrugged, then heard a sound from the other direction. It was Lisa, tapping on the glass on the passenger side. Reluctantly, Evan pushed the button that rolled that window down.

"I'm not allowed in the street," she informed him.

"I see."

"Why are you sitting here?"

"I'm waiting."

"For Marla Simone?" Brian asked.

"Yeah."

"My mom says you're leaving soon."

Evan nodded, then winced at the way his head hurt. "In about three minutes."

Lisa gripped the car door with her small fingers and rested her chin on her knuckles. "Mommy was sad last night."

"Was she?"

"She was watching a movie, one of those kissing ones, and her face looked like this. You know—" Lisa's eyebrows took on a tragic curve and her small pink mouth turned downward at both edges. "Like that."

Evan bit down a smile. "That's pretty sad."

Brian turned to his friends. "You guys wanna play some ball?"

"Me too!" Lisa shouted, her high voice cutting through Evan's head like a soprano buzz saw. "Mommy says you have to take me too!"

With much whooping and hollering, the children raced off down the block. And then they were gone. Evan closed his eyes again, surprised to find himself, in spite of his throbbing head, chuckling just a little. They sure were nice kids. He didn't know a lot of children—his friends generally weren't family types—but from what he could tell, Chris was a hell of a good mother.

A woman with children—another fine reason he and Chris should stay far away from each other. Kids meant problems, and who needed any more problems?

He heard Chris's front door close and waited for the sound of Marla's heels on the sidewalk, closely followed by the smell of the very expensive French perfume she wore. Chris's smell was more natural, fresh—warm and lemony, like sunshine and soap.

Like the fragrance that was drifting past his nostrils just then.

Evan sat up straight just as the passenger door opened and Chris slid into the seat. Her face was solemn, bereft of makeup or anything resembling her natural vivacity.

"Hi," she said softly.

"Hello."

"Marla is what we euphemistically call 'freshening up,' so I told her I wanted to say good-bye to you."

"You turned her down, I trust."

"Quite definitively . . . I hope."

His mouth quirked up knowingly. "Then Marla is not really freshening up; she's giving me one last shot at getting you to change your mind."

"Oh."

"Which I'm not even going to bother with."

"Thank you."

Chris twisted her hands in her lap and studied a spot

on the dashboard. "I wanted to thank you . . . and to apologize for yesterday."

"No need."

"Yes, there is. I was pretty shaken, in case you couldn't tell. I hadn't realized how much I needed to talk about . . . about that night."

"I gathered as much."

She ventured a glance at him. His face was set in a stern, unsmiling cast. He was a little frightening. "I wasn't myself," she explained.

"I see. Then it wasn't you who kissed me like that, it was some other woman."

His bitterness stung her, and she looked down at her lap.

He put his hand on her wrist, then removed it quickly. "Look," he said, less brittle now. "You don't owe me any explanations, or any apologies. We both got a little carried away, that's all. You were vulnerable, and I was, I don't know, involved in your story. We were 'swept up in the passion of the moment,' as they say in the movies. That's all."

Chris directed her gaze out the window, unwilling to have him see the way his blithe assessment had affected her. She could feel a few tears gathering under her lower lids, and she didn't really want to encourage them.

Several moments passed in silence before Evan spoke. "Why is your life a lie?"

She'd wondered if he'd bring up what she'd said yesterday, and here it was. Her response was to keep her eyes averted from him and shake her head.

More silent moments slid by before he said, "So, then, I guess we won't be seeing each other anymore."

She swallowed down another wave of emotion, wishing all her feelings weren't so close to the surface this morning. Forcing herself to face him again, she managed to bring up a small smile. "I guess we won't. You were wonderful to me yesterday, and I'll never forget you."

The curve of his answering smile was cynical. "Never say never. Shall we shake hands and say good-bye?"

She looked down at the broad, tanned hand he offered and remembered how good it had felt to have both his hands stroking her yesterday, healing her with their strength. She hesitated for a moment, then grasped his hand quickly and let it go just as quickly.

"Good-bye," she said, then let herself out of the car.

Marla was emerging from the house as Chris walked resolutely up the path. "Good-bye, Chris," the actress called out cheerfully.

Chris nodded, then pushed open her front door and disappeared inside.

"Are you in a better mood?" Marla asked Evan as she settled herself into her seat.

He was no longer angry, that was for sure. But he was still in the dark about Chris's actions, and overcome by a strong sense of desolation. Damn. He preferred the anger.

"Moderately," he answered.

"Good. Let's go."

Evan fired up the engine, then ventured a last look toward the house.

Chris stood in the window, the curtains parted just

enough so that Evan could see her but not read the expression on her face. After a moment she raised a hand and waved once. He stared at her for another couple of seconds, then waved back. He watched as the curtains draped back into place. She was gone.

After checking his side mirror, Evan drove off down the street. It really was for the best, he told himself. Sure, there was an attraction there, but there were problems too. Chris wasn't the kind of woman a man had a quick affair with, and that was the only kind of relationship Evan allowed himself, wasn't it? Besides, she didn't want him. Hell, she'd told him to get lost. He was glad he was saying good-bye to Loman. Damned glad.

Marla heaved a sigh, and he glanced over at her. "Tough session at the negotiating table?"

"You were right," she said. "Chris said no. Again."

"And did you finally hear it?"

She slanted him a disbelieving look and grinned. "Are you kidding? I'll get her. Just you wait." She turned back and focused her determined gaze somewhere beyond the windshield. "Just you wait."

"Damn."

Evan hated when the phone rang while he was working at his home office. He'd been hired to do a quick, uncredited fix on a murder mystery script and had been staring out the window at the brown hillsides of Malibu, looking for inspiration. Just as he'd been on the verge of cracking the back of a particularly difficult plot point concerning a disappearing body, the phone jangled insistently. He'd forgotten to turn it off and let the machine get it, the way he usually did when he was working.

He saved the words on his computer screen before he picked up the receiver and mumbled, "Yes?"

"Evan, I got it!"

"Who is this?"

"Marla, you idiot."

"Okay, you got what?"

"The rights! Chris McConnell—she's letting me do her story!"

Something in the vicinity of Evan's stomach did a quick backflip. "Are you serious?"

"Sure am," Marla said smugly. "I have an exclusive!"

Chris. Just the sound of her name might have brightened his mood, except that the meaning of Marla's words registered. Disappointment hit. She'd caved in. A mere two weeks after saying no and really—he'd have taken bets on it—meaning it. Fool that he was, he'd thought he'd met a woman who couldn't be bought. Right.

What had Marla offered her? he wondered. Probably money and plenty of it. Enough, finally, so that Chris could bury any lingering objections. Another one fallen by the wayside. Seduced by money and the phony glamour of "Hollywood."

"Chris will be out here next week," Marla said. "I'm putting her up for four days at the Bel Age so we can get some deep background on her."

Chris was coming here, to L.A.! He felt his damn heart lifting again at the thought. For two weeks he'd been unable to get her out of his mind. Nights of sleeplessness had been followed by furious rides at dawn on his horse and distracted, unproductive days. And now she was actually coming here, to the West Coast.

"I assume you're still interested in the script and coproduction deal," Marla said.

"I don't know."

"What do you mean, you don't know?"

"Just what I said. I'm working on a couple of other projects, Marla."

"Cancel them. We have a green light at the studio. Your agent can ask for top dollar, but don't tell them I said so. I want you to write me a fantastic role, Evan, the way only you can. . . ."

She went on babbling about herself and the part, self-obsessed as usual. Me me me. Marla sounded like so many of the others—addicted to attention and power and money, trying to fill a hole in their emotions that couldn't really ever be filled. It happened to most of the women in this town.

It had happened to his ex-wife.

Sue Ann and he had been sweethearts all their lives in that small Wyoming hellhole he'd called his hometown. Evan's mother—the only softness he'd ever known—abandoned her family when he was six, his brother was five, and his father was rip-roaring drunk, as usual. Sue Ann's family had been like his, never having enough money or smarts or dreams. The two of them used to vow that as soon as they could, they would escape. Together.

He was nineteen and she was seventeen when they ran off to Las Vegas, got married, and wound up on the West Coast. Within a year he was working two minimum-wage jobs and enrolled in a writing internship program at one of the studios. Sue Ann, in the meantime, young and beautiful and too trusting, got caught up in the fast lane . . . and the drugs. By the following year she was gone, out of Evan's life—off to Europe with a so-called producer whose sideline consisted of supplying nose candy to half the industry.

He'd seen her once more, a few years later, to sign divorce papers. She was still beautiful, but seemed used up and lifeless. He was glad to find out he was over her; he was also cured of expectations in the love department.

Which was why he kept all his affairs short and sweet. He didn't trust easily, if at all. He was aware that he'd grown hard, that calluses had developed in the region of his heart. And most of the time he didn't care. He had his work, his friends, and a life that was a hell of a lot better than he'd even known existed back in the days of the dry, dusty Wyoming summers.

And then, a couple of weeks earlier, Chris McConnell entered his life. And suddenly his day-to-day existence no longer seemed quite so full, so satisfying. And now she was coming here, to his stomping grounds.

And he was damned if he knew how to react to the news.

Chris peered out the window at the colorful shops along Melrose Avenue and at the throngs of teenagers on the street. They seemed impossibly young and trying too hard not to look it, with their black, angry clothing and bizarre haircuts. She'd been that young once, she supposed, but it felt like a lifetime ago. She wished her anxiety weren't interfering with this movie buff's dream adventure. If only . . .

She'd flown to Los Angeles the previous evening. First class. Wide seats and service befitting royalty. It had been her virgin airplane flight; her previous traveling had been via Greyhound buses and cars. When John and she had married, he'd promised her a trip, a long trip, "one of these days," but they'd never gotten around to it.

What a hick she was, she thought ruefully. Twenty-eight years old and she'd never been on an airplane, never seen the ocean.

The driver who had met her at the airport had handled her luggage and whisked her along the L.A. freeway system into Beverly Hills. There she'd been given an incredible hotel room with a walk-in closet and her very own thick terry-cloth robe with the name of the hotel embroidered across the pocket.

Now, here she was on a sunny morning, being spirited east on Melrose toward Hollywood and a famous film-history-drenched studio. To "take a meeting," as they said. The whole thing was like a dream.

And even better, Evan would be there.

Her heart sped up at the thought of seeing him again, then she admonished herself. Nothing had changed. If only . . .

If only all of this could have been accomplished in some way other than blackmail.

Marla had called last week, starting out the conversation with a generous monetary offer, including a donation to the town library and a college trust fund for Chris's children. It had been really tempting, but once again Chris had said no.

Then the actress had dropped the bombshell: A detective had done some research into Chris's past, and he'd uncovered "a few little discrepancies." For instance, Chris McConnell wasn't her real name, was it? Yes, yes, it was her married name for sure, but her maiden name— Christine Day—wasn't her real name either. There were a few more details, should Chris care to hear them. Little tidbits about time spent in a juvenile facility, even a question or two about Brian's *real* father.

Marla certainly didn't want Chris to get the impression that she was holding any of that over her head, she assured her sweetly. But surely Chris would want to come to L.A. and "discuss it"?

After that there hadn't been a choice. Swallowing down her anger at Marla, Chris agreed to come. Dora was pretty emphatic in her disapproval, but finally threw her hands up in the air, saying she would care for the children.

Chris turned down an offer from Frank Metzger to be sent off to L.A. with a parade. She used some of the advance money Marla sent to buy a few new articles of clothing and boarded the plane with a trepidation that had nothing to do with a fear of flying.

As she waved good-bye to her children, all she could think about was that years ago she'd taken refuge with John McConnell and had made a safe life for herself in Loman. But flying out of the airport, she couldn't shake the feeling that her sense of security was about to come to an end.

Now, as the car glided through the old wrought iron gates of Paramount Studios, Chris the movie buff wished this could be happening without all the attendant tension.

On the other hand, she reminded herself—and her heart expanded at the thought—in a few moments Chris the woman would be seeing Evan again.

SIX

"Chris! How good to see you!"

Marla was all smiles as she held out two perfectly manicured hands to Chris, like a gracious hostess welcoming someone to a cocktail party. The actress was wearing a long, form-fitting green sweater that came to mid-thigh, black leggings, and high-heeled suede boots. The sweater matched her eyes, which danced with vibrancy.

Chris felt decidedly unglamorous next to Marla, even though her own outfit was certainly several notches above the usual blouse and skirt she wore back home. However, she reminded herself, she wasn't there to wear a dazzling wardrobe, or to compete with Marla; Chris's task was to keep her wits about her while giving Marla just enough information to make her go away. Please.

"Hello, Marla," Chris said, her voice pleasantly neutral and her hands firmly wrapped around her clutch purse. She would have much preferred to have been greeted by Evan, but he didn't seem to be anywhere in sight. She swallowed down a wave of disappointment as she stood in the doorway, her gaze sweeping past Marla into the room beyond.

The large reception area had several closed doors leading off into other rooms—other offices, she imagined. One door, partially opened, revealed a good-size kitchen. To Chris's right was a glass-topped desk, behind which sat a plain young woman typing into a computer. Much of the floor space was taken up with oversize expensive-looking couches and easy chairs in soft beige with white stripes, glass coffee tables, and tasteful southwestern-style art on the walls. The whole room was decorated like something out of a magazine.

A man rose from one of the couches and came toward Chris. He was portly and nearly bald, and what was left of his hair was pulled back in a gray ponytail. Marla grabbed his elbow and said, "Herb, meet Chris McConnell. Chris, this is Herb Davis. He'll be writing the script."

"Writing the script?" Chris repeated, startled. Wasn't Evan supposed to be writing the script? He was the producer, she knew that. Producer-writer; a hyphenate, as they said here in Los Angeles. From her faithful reading of *Premiere* magazine, she knew there were often several writers on every script. Maybe Herb would be doing the first draft and Evan would come in for the second or third draft? Chris didn't want to ask Marla to explain, not in front of Herb, just in case her assumptions were off base. She'd wait and see what developed.

As Chris shook Herb's hand, Marla said, "You don't

need to stand in the doorway, you know. Come on in, Chris. Can I offer you anything? A drink? Soda? Coffee?"

Chris could tell from the way Marla was fussing that she was raring to go. Her nerves were fairly humming out loud.

"No, thanks. I'm not thirsty." Chris took a few steps into the room, unable to avoid the feeling of entering the den of a dangerous jungle animal with only a small chair available for defensive purposes.

"Are you sure? Judy can get it for you." Marla's head indicated the young typist, who glanced up at the mention of her name.

"Do you need me, Ms. Simone?"

"Chris?" Marla said again.

"Nothing, thanks."

"Maybe you're hungry? We can send out for anything you want. Ever had sushi? We have the greatest little Japanese place—"

"No, thanks, Marla. Really," Chris said as emphatically as she could. The woman simply did not know how to deal with being turned down—about anything, it seemed. "I've eaten already."

Rubbing her hands together, Marla walked over to the desk, then picked up a small tape recorder. "All right, then, let's get down to work. We'll be taping our discussions, of course."

Chris frowned. "What exactly am I supposed to talk about?"

"Gut stuff, you know. The inside you, real emotions." Marla's expressions and gestures turned theatrically serious as she went on. "The terror you felt that night. The way your life was affected, changed forever. Some memories of your childhood, your kids, your late husband, how it was between the two of you." She grinned happily. "All the little intimate stuff of your daily life."

Slowly, Chris sank onto a couch, staring at Marla, and felt her spirit plummeting to her ankles. This was going to be a nightmare, an absolute nightmare.

And there was no Evan standing by to rescue her.

Evan was disgusted with himself.

He was pacing. Pacing, for Pete's sake, and he was not the kind of man who paced. But that's what he was doing, one agitated step after another across his office floor, checking the time on his watch every fifteen seconds or so.

She would have landed the evening before and spent the night at the hotel. Even though he wasn't the writer on Marla's project—he'd decided it was best to turn the job down—he'd managed to find out the details of Chris's itinerary. The name of the airline, the time of landing and departure, what room she was staying in.

He knew Herb Davis was doing the script. Herb was a decent writer; he would do a good job. If she could keep Marla from eating her alive, Chris would probably survive the experience.

So why was he wearing grooves in the braided rug next to his desk, and why was his black Lab, Buster, looking up at him with puzzlement, dog-style? Considering that he'd had too little sleep over the past two weeks, Evan was amazed at the excess energy coursing through

•

his body. There was a kind of buzzing throughout his bloodstream. He simply couldn't sit still.

He'd spent the morning trying to work on the mystery rewrite, but he couldn't make his fingers behave on the keys. He was a pro, nothing and no one ever kept him from his work—he'd met deadlines with high fever, after all-night poker games, even through the pain of a dislocated shoulder.

But not today. There would be no working today.

He muttered an oath. Might as well go for a ride, he thought. Saddle up Fancy Man or Chester and gallop the tension out. His horses had been getting more workouts than usual lately, he thought ruefully.

As Evan was heading for the door of his office, the phone rang. It sounded so shrill. He stopped in his tracks and stared at the instrument perched on his desk. He would let the machine get it. But he would listen in, just in case.

His outgoing message was followed by two short beeps. "Evan, if you're there, pick up." It was Marla, whispering loudly and sounding highly impatient. "I said pick up the damn phone."

He forced a couple of calming breaths in and out of his nostrils before he lifted the receiver and put it to his ear. "What's up?" he asked with what he hoped was casual indifference.

"She doesn't trust us, Evan. We're pumping her with questions and she answers with one word. Yes. No. Maybe. I'm in my private office now. She can't hear me."

There was no need to ask who *she* was. "I see."

"Herb is doing his best, but it's a disaster."

"Is it."

"I'll double your usual price if you'll get over here right now."

He didn't answer.

"She's mentioned your name twice. I've been avoiding telling her the truth. Evan, this is important to me. Don't make me beg. Please."

Hesitating, he closed his eyes for a moment. Then he shook his head with a self-mocking smile. Why was he bothering? There really was no choice in the matter, was there? Some things were inevitable.

"I'll be there in forty-five minutes."

He pulled the Ranger into a visitor space, leapt out of the car, and dashed up the stairs to Marla's office. The door was slightly ajar, but before he went in he took a moment to compose himself, raking his fingers through his hair and adjusting his shirt collar. Then he chuckled quietly at his jumpiness, at his need to make a good impression on the woman inside the room.

He eased the door open and was greeted by a sight more welcome than he'd ever imagined.

Chris.

She was alone in the large room, perched on the edge of a couch, her clasped hands resting on her knees. Her eyes were closed and her mouth was in a stern line, as though she were praying but doubted anyone was listening. Her entire being radiated tension, and he wondered, for the umpteenth time, why she'd given in and said yes to Marla.

She wore a cornflower-blue silk dress and high heels, and her hair flowed around her shoulders in soft waves. She looked professional and businesslike, very feminine and subtly alluring—nothing like the Midwest mom straight out of a peanut butter commercial whom he'd met a couple of weeks before.

In all his years in L.A., he'd seen and bedded women more beautiful and more well endowed, but never had any caused the breath to leave his body the way this woman did. Just what was it about her, he wondered, that called to him so strongly, that made him feel like he was returning home after a long journey?

"Chris," he said softly.

Her eyes snapped open and she turned her head toward him. Then she smiled at him, her lips parting slightly. "Hi, Evan."

Nothing had changed. That throaty voice of hers could still melt his bones.

"Welcome to my world," he said.

"I thought you weren't going to be here."

He leaned against the doorframe and draped his arms across his chest. "You thought wrong."

"But Marla said—"

"Did I hear my name?" Marla chirped, coming into the room from one of the other offices. Chris turned toward the actress, and Evan observed how the tension returned to Chris's face again.

"Just what did Marla say?" he asked.

"That you were too busy and that Herb—" Chris stopped, her confusion apparent, and looked around the room. "What happened to Herb?"

"He was only a stand-in," Marla said blithely. "Evan's here now and we can get started."

"Stand-in?"

"And he got paid very well for an hour's work. So here we go." She picked up the small tape recorder that was lying on the desk and punched in the record button. After setting it down on the coffee table in front of Chris, Marla returned to the desk and leaned a hip against the edge, smiling in encouragement.

Marla's flurry of activity earned her a look from Chris that could be described only as distrustful. A person would have to be deprived of all five senses, Evan thought, to miss the strained interactions between the two women. Just what was going on?

Chris pointed to the tape recorder. "I told you I'm not comfortable with that thing. I mean, I'm not sure I can spill my guts into a machine."

Marla waved her hand impatiently. "Just pretend it's not there. Come on, Chris, you can pretend, can't you?"

Evan unfolded his arms and walked into the room. "No, you don't have to 'spill your guts,' " he said to Chris. "Not in the least. We can start out just talking. Marla, turn the recorder off."

"But—"

He whipped his head around and stared her down. "I said, turn it off."

She did.

He looked at Chris, whose stiff posture and facial expression telegraphed a woman holding a tight rein on her anger. Sending a message of reassurance to her with his eyes, Evan settled himself next to her on the couch, keeping a few feet between them so she wouldn't feel crowded. Angling his body toward her, he propped one bent leg on a thick cushion, patting his shirt pocket absently as he did.

"You can smoke if you want," Chris said. "I don't mind."

His mouth quirked up. "I can't. I quit."

"Good for you."

"I miss it like hell."

She nodded. "I know what you mean."

He draped his arm over the back of the couch. "You used to be a smoker? How long's it been?"

"Three, almost four years now." The belligerent set of Chris's posture eased somewhat as she faced him, pointedly ignoring Marla's presence at the desk behind her. "I stopped when I got pregnant with Lisa. I'd just read an article about brain damage or something horrible that could happen to fetuses from smoking, and it really scared me."

"Yeah, I imagine it did. You're that kind of mother."

She cocked her head to one side. "What kind is that?"

"The kind that takes it seriously. Who doesn't think of kids as a pain in the butt. Not all that common anymore." Unbidden early memories of his own mother and her warmth flooded his brain for the first time in a long while. He shifted in his seat, uncomfortable with the sense of melancholy that came over him. "You know, committed."

"I guess I am that, for sure, but I have a feeling it's more common than you think. We read only about the aberrations, you know, not the norm. It makes for more exciting newscasts."

"You might be right at that. Whew. I feel better for the future of the country already."

She smiled at his sardonic remark and he returned the smile, enjoying once again the sheer pleasure of Chris's company, and the easy banter they seemed to fall into without effort.

Marla coughed, and Evan glanced over at her, raising his eyebrows. "Yes, Marla?"

"Nothing. Ignore me. You're doing fine."

"Thank you," he said wryly. He regarded Chris; it was obvious that she was much more at ease now. He leaned into her slightly, meeting her gray-eyed gaze. "You okay?"

She nodded.

"Want to get a little work done?"

"I guess we'd better."

She grinned at him, the full-wattage version that was enough to illuminate a room, and he almost expelled an audible breath.

"I mean," she said, "I *did* agree to do this."

Why? he wanted to say, but didn't.

"We can start with the simple stuff," he said. "You know, where and when you were born. The basics."

Chris knew that the silence that followed his innocent question could be described only as loaded. She had, up until that point, been unsure about just what parts of the truth she could tell. Now it seemed—if she wanted to avoid getting tangled up in a web of lies and confusion— she was going to have to tell pretty much all of it.

Up to a point.

"I'm not sure where or when I was born," she began.

"Excuse me?"

"I'm an orphan. A foundling, actually, left on the steps of a clinic for unwed mothers. In Chicago."

"This is terrific!" Marla said from her perch on the edge of the desk. "Great beginning."

Evan slanted her a look of reproach. "Marla, did anyone ever tell you that you have the sensitivity of a sledgehammer?"

Chris allowed herself to chuckle for the first time that morning. It was because Evan was there; he'd changed the entire day for her just by walking into the room. He would rein in Marla's enthusiasm, would make the interview process tolerable. Chris was even beginning to understand that Marla's cavalier treatment of her wasn't personal. The actress was obsessed, totally career-driven, and would allow nothing and no one to get in her way.

Now, with Evan sitting right beside her, this whole nightmare might be somewhat pleasant. She'd seen the welcome in his eyes, that he liked seeing her as much as she liked seeing him. That wonderful lime aftershave was uncluttered by the odor of cigarettes she associated with him in her memory. Her ex-smoking knight in shining armor, she thought, although he would probably hate that description.

"But, Evan," Marla was saying, walking back and forth near the couch. "Think of the visuals. An orphan, left on the steps, abandoned. Maybe the opening shot, before the credits. A chilly Chicago winter, a tiny baby, wrapped tightly, crying from the cold. Snowflakes on its face. The camera pulls back to bare trees, a scrap of paper being chased down the street by a gust of wind . . ."

"All that's missing is a skinny, one-eyed mutt sniffing at the basket," he said sarcastically. "Or the lonely howl of a wolf."

"It was summer, actually," Chris said. Both Evan and Marla looked at her. "Sorry."

His mouth turned up in appreciation and she smiled back at him. "Scratch one opening shot of snow," he said.

"Who cares what month it was?" Marla said. "It's still great drama."

Chris nodded. "I know. I'm afraid a lot of my early childhood is straight out of Dickens."

"See?" Marla said in triumph, then plopped down on the chair adjacent to Chris and gazed at her eagerly. "Go on. Tell us what happened next."

Now Evan was on one side of her and Marla on the other. Chris had to fight down the feeling of being closed in, and made a concentrated effort to relax. She turned to Marla, determined to cooperate. She'd agreed to this, and she always tried to honor her agreements.

"I was placed in a foster home," she said in as matter-of-fact a tone as she could manage. "I stayed there for a couple of years. I was, apparently, pretty sickly. A lot of colds, a few bouts with pneumonia. Of course, I don't actually remember any of this," she said with a small smile, "but it was in my records."

"Were you adopted?" Evan asked.

That question made Chris look down at her lap. The old hurt of not being chosen, not being special enough, was coming up again. Don't show vulnerability, she told herself. Not now.

"I was not only pretty sickly as a child," she said, picking an imaginary piece of lint off her dress, "but I was also shy, very shy. No, I was never adopted."

"How many foster homes did you live in?"

Marla asked that question, and Chris made herself look straight at her. "Ten," she said with another shrug. "Twelve. I don't really remember."

"Where did you go to school?" Evan asked.

She knew her expression was guarded, but then, she wasn't as good at masking her emotions with Evan. "Which grades?"

"How about high school?" Marla said.

Chris faced the actress again and allowed herself another small smile. "I went to four high schools, a new one each year." She looked at Evan. "And I never graduated."

Marla moved to the edge of her chair. "But you're a teacher. That takes a college degree."

"Sure does," she said. "I took a high school equivalency test before I began college." She turned her attention in the other direction—toward Evan—one more time. "I went to night school for a while, then full-time. And got my degree that way."

"Nothing came easily, did it?" Evan said quietly. "It must have been tough. But you got through it. Marla?" he went on without looking at the actress. "Why don't you let me ask the questions? We don't want to give Chris whiplash."

Marla frowned, but sat back in her chair.

Good, Chris thought. Keep the woman away from me.

Evan looked at Chris encouragingly. "Give us a sense of place, okay? For instance—the foundling incident. That was Chicago, right? Is that where you grew up?"

Chronologically, the questions were getting closer to the years she would rather skip over, so she chose her words with care. "The rest of my childhood was spent in various towns in Illinois."

"And college?" Evan asked.

"That was in Boulder. In Colorado."

"I see. Is that where you met your husband?"

"Yes."

"How?" Marla said.

Evan shot her a quelling look. "How?" he said to Chris. "If you met in an unusual or funny way, we might be able to use it in the script."

Chris relaxed her shoulders a little. They'd just passed over the difficult years; maybe everything would be all right after all. *Please, let it be all right.*

"I was working as a server at one of the dorm cafeterias," she said. "That was my morning job—at night I waited tables in town. Anyway, a hot tin of scrambled eggs slipped out of my hands and splattered all over one of the graduate students—John McConnell. I was terrified that I would lose my job, but he—John—was very nice about it." She lifted her hands, palms up, then dropped them back to her lap. "And that's how we met."

Marla clapped enthusiastically. "Cute. Great scene, huh, Evan? Terrific background stuff." She favored Chris with a happy grin. "See? This isn't so bad, is it?"

"Not so far," Chris answered Marla.

Evan noticed the look that was exchanged between the two women, speculative on Marla's part, and something else—a warning?—on Chris's. Don't push it, the look said.

Marla glanced at her watch, jumped up from the chair, and smoothed her sweater over her hips, managing to draw attention to the generous curves of her diminutive body. If that little gesture had been for him, Evan thought, she was wasting her time. Chris McConnell— with her innate classiness and modesty, her lack of artifice —had it all over the actress in every area.

"Well," Marla said. "I have to get out of here. I have an interview to give *TV Guide*. I'm going to talk up our project. Isn't that wonderful?"

"I can't remember when I've ever felt so excited," Chris deadpanned.

Evan burst out laughing. Marla seemed momentarily annoyed. She picked up her purse from the desk and went over to the door. With a look that was cheerful and sly at the same time, she said, "Chris, I leave you in Evan's very capable hands. Evan, do whatever you have to, but write me a wonderful script, all right? Bye, you two."

After Marla sailed out the door, the room's ambience changed to one of calm. Evan watched as Chris took a deep breath and closed her eyes, as if she'd just that moment become aware of how tightly she'd been clenching all her muscles in Marla's presence. It hadn't escaped his attention that all through the interview, even when Chris seemed to be answering the questions with ease, her hands had been locked together in her lap.

"How are you holding up?"

Her eyes snapped open at his quiet question, and she sighed. "Fine, I guess. Except, in case you can't tell, I don't want to be here."

"Gee, you coulda fooled me."

"Yeah, I don't hide my emotions too well, do I?"

"Oh, you do okay." He studied her for a moment, frowning.

A couple of weeks earlier, when he'd held Chris in his arms as she sobbed, she'd allowed him a glimpse of the emotional scarring inside, but only a brief one. Most of the time, in spite of her own assessment, she was an expert in masking her pain. Not today. He'd heard a lot of anguish today, and it was not only troubling, but he was having a hell of a time keeping editorial distance.

How rough it must have been for her, moving not only from house to house, but family to family. Never keeping the same friends, or siblings, or the same bedroom. For all the drawbacks of his own childhood, there'd been consistency at least, a routine, the same bed to sleep in every night, a brother to play and fight with, a school that all the kids in town went to. The church, the neighborhood grocery store, the baseball field. The familiar things of a normal life.

No matter how tangled or distorted that life might have been.

"Evan?"

He snapped his attention back to the present. "Sorry. I was mulling something over."

"Getting ideas for the script?"

"In a way."

"You can turn that thing on." She pointed to the tape recorder still resting on the coffee table. "If you want to."

He regarded her for a moment, then said, "I have a better idea. Come on."

He rose from the couch, grabbed her hand, and pulled her with him toward the door.

"Where are we going?"

"You've never seen the ocean, right?" he asked with a smile.

"Right."

"One ocean view, coming up."

SEVEN

He drove them south from Hollywood, along busy city streets and onto the Santa Monica Freeway heading west. Chris couldn't see much of the landscape due to the high walls of the freeway, but the blue sky seemed to have an overlay of whitewash, making the color a lot less vivid than the sky above Loman. Evan pointed out Century City, a collection of offices, shops, and hotels built on the old Fox backlot.

Backlot. Chris liked the sound of that word. She was here finally, close by the land of dreams and imagination, of make-believe and happy endings.

They didn't talk much; she was too busy looking around. She glanced over at Evan from time to time, liking the feeling of sitting next to him in a car, windows open, her hair blowing around her face. He too seemed more relaxed now, away from the office, away from Marla. He drove easily and expertly, one elbow propped on the door, his other hand—broad and strong—on the steering wheel.

She found her attention drawn to his hand and the way his long fingers were both callused and artistic-looking at the same time. She imagined that hand stroking her, making flesh-to-flesh contact, just the edge of a fingernail along her wrist bone or his palm resting lightly on her shoulder. She was strangely shy in this fantasy about being the one to initiate anything, remembering the barriers between them the last time they sat next to each other in a car, outside her house in Loman, when they said good-bye.

They drove through Santa Monica, then into a tunnel. When they came out the other side, there on Chris's left was the Pacific Ocean.

"Oh," she gasped when she saw it. "Oh, it's lovely."

Because the autumn day was sunny, the color of the water was mostly a pale turquoise, with darker gray-green strips near the shoreline. The sun glittered over it all like tiny spotlights. As far as the eye could see there were huge expanses of white beach, broken up by lifeguard stations, parking lots, telephone wires, the occasional small building. There was a bike path along the highway and a sight she was already used to—palm trees.

Out the right side of the car Chris could see mountains, some overgrown with shrubbery, brown from the recent summer sun, some dotted with houses built at all kinds of crazy angles. But it was the view out Evan's window that called to her. The ocean. Sailboats in the distance and, closer in, swimmers and some kids on surfboards. At the shoreline a toddler played with a pail and shovel while a grown-up kept a close watch on the waves.

The wind continued to ruffle Chris's hair, the sun shone on her through the window of Evan's Ranger, and she found herself able to put away the feeling of dread that she'd had since Marla's phone call. A laugh bubbled up out of nowhere.

"Oh, Evan," she said, turning to him with a happy grin. "It's just like in the movies." When he chuckled, she felt herself flush at how ingenuous she must sound. "I mean, it's breathtaking, really it is. And I knew it would be."

"Want to take a little walk on the sand?"

"Oh, yes."

He swung the car into a nearly deserted parking lot. "We're lucky it's October. During the summer, this time of day you couldn't get near here."

He pulled into a space and turned off the engine. Then he reached across her and opened the door for her. The way her body responded to his body's proximity, even for that brief moment, took her by surprise, and she found herself needing to hold herself still for a couple of seconds so she could gather her wits.

Evan pulled at the latch of his door. "Let's do it," he said.

"I just remembered that I'm wearing nylons and heels."

"Take 'em off."

"But—"

"Hey, you're in L.A. now," he said with a crooked

grin. "The only dress code we subscribe to is 'anything goes.' "

He hopped out of the car and turned his back to her, directing his gaze toward the water. Chris felt grateful to him for his discretion. She kicked off her high heels and, checking to make sure no one was watching, reached up under her dress and rolled down her panty hose, pulling them over her toes and folding the garment neatly next to her shoes. Now she was wearing only a silk bra and matching half slip under her dress—new purchases that had been wickedly extravagant and felt soft and cool against her skin. With her bare legs and bare bottom, she felt deliciously sinful. How easy it was, she thought ruefully, to throw caution and midwest modesty to the wind.

"Can I leave my purse in the car?"

Evan turned around and leaned in. "Sure thing. I'll lock up."

She joined him on his side of the car, and together they walked down toward the shoreline. Without her shoes on, he seemed so very tall. And still heart-stoppingly sexy. Tight, faded jeans outlined the contours of his slim yet muscular thighs. A pale blue V-neck sweater hugged the broad expanse of his shoulders and revealed dark, curly chest hair against skin that, like his face and hands, was golden-brown from the sun.

At the edge of the water he turned a slow smile on Chris, the laugh lines around his eyes deepening. As she gazed at him, the sky and the ocean a backdrop to the rugged picture he presented, a fleeting wisp of memory tugged at her brain. She forced herself to concentrate until she captured it. Of course, she thought. The last time she'd had this kind of reaction to a man—a combination of heated blood and trepidation, and the unseemly urge to giggle—had been years earlier in a three-for-a-dollar movie theater. The film had been *Lifeguard*; the moment Sam Elliot, in his tight, narrow swimsuit, had come running out of the water, Chris had lost her prepubescent heart.

Evan reminded her of the actor—broad and brown from the sun, a frontier cowboy reluctantly transplanted to the late twentieth century. Even his voice recalled Sam Elliot's—its low western twang an invitation to secret, unimaginable delights.

They strolled along the beach, the waves coming in and foaming around Chris's feet. She lifted her face to the afternoon sun, loving the salt smell and relishing the way her toes curled in the cool, soft sand.

After a while Evan glanced over at her and offered his hand. She hesitated a moment, then took it. Fingers entwined, they continued on. She had no idea how much time passed. The occasional shell caught her eye, and she tugged on his hand to stop so she could pick up a particularly pretty one. When she showed it to him with wonder, he smiled at her enthusiasm.

"Am I being silly?" she asked.

"Not in the least. I take seashells for granted after all these years." He raised his free hand to her face, stroking one long finger along the contour of her cheek. "You make me remember."

She swallowed down a sigh at his touch, then Evan squeezed her hand once again and they walked on. After a few moments he shook his head slowly. "I can't get over the fact that you've never seen the ocean."

"There's never been enough money to travel, that's all."

"What did your husband do?"

Evan wished he could take it back, because the feeling of ease between them faded as Chris withdrew her hand from his. "I guess we're working on the script now. You're trying to find out more about me."

"Yeah. But not for the script, for myself."

She turned her gaze on him, then raised an eyebrow. "Maybe both, huh. It's so beautiful here, I don't really want to talk about myself. But I guess I'd better readjust my thinking."

"You don't have to."

"Sure I do. That's why I came, isn't it?"

She was right, of course. They were working now, even though he'd rather be exploring a . . . what? A friendship? Relationship? A roll in the hay? What word could describe what he and Chris were to each other?

For a while as they walked along, she seemed to focus her gaze on the curving coastline. "John wound up in business with his father," she told him in that same even tone she'd used back in Marla's office. "They were accountants, but never had much of a practice. It helped that we all lived together, but their clients were small farmers and always in financial trouble. My salary from teaching school came in pretty handy, and we always had food on the table and clothes to wear and a roof over our heads. But travel was considered a luxury, that's all."

"When did he die?"

"Two and a half years ago. It was pretty rough for a while."

Words of condolence came to mind, but instead, after a brief silence, he surprised himself by asking, "Was it a good marriage?"

The question seemed to stop her. Looking down, she carved patterns in the sand with her toes. "I suppose it was. We each offered something the other needed. Which I think is a good thing in a marriage."

Evan wanted to ask what those missing qualities were, and why he sensed there had been no passion in her married life. He wanted, in fact, to know why she had withdrawn from him, as though pulling a cloak over her. What secrets was she hiding? He needed to know everything about her. The script would be better if he did, he told himself.

How could he gain her trust? he wondered, because he was determined to do just that. Not for the first time Evan wished that they'd met under different circumstances.

But with the drastic dissimilarities between her world and his, he couldn't imagine any other way they might have met.

Holding her elbow, he pointed toward a far point on the horizon. "You can't tell today, but out there lies the famous Catalina island."

She smiled. " 'Twenty-six Miles Across the Sea.' "

"It's a nice one-day sail. If you were staying longer, we could—" He broke off his train of thought. "Just how long are you planning on staying?"

"Till Sunday morning."

He frowned. "Today's Wednesday. That gives us only a few days."

"For the script?"

He looked deep in her eyes. "For a lot of things."

She didn't look away, but he could see several warring emotions flicker across her face. Pleasure at his words, some fear. Curiosity. Desire too. Oh, yeah, that was for sure. She wanted him as much as he wanted her, but she wasn't sure just what to do about it.

He wouldn't push, he told himself. The hunger he felt for her was always there, just below the surface, but it would stay below the surface. For the moment.

"Want to sit down for a while?" he said. "Maybe watch the waves and talk?"

She nodded and they made their way over to a wooden bench at the edge of the sand. The beach was deserted except for the occasional jogger running along the coastline. He slung an arm on the back of the bench, not quite touching her.

Chris raised her face to the sun for a couple of moments, then turned and smiled at him. "I didn't know. I honestly didn't know."

"What?" He touched some of the pale hair that curled around her shoulder.

"That there could be something this quiet, this beautiful, this perfect. It's the strangest feeling. I've never seen the ocean, never been near one before, but I know it from my dreams. And it's even better than my dreams."

He sifted the golden strands between his fingers. "Tell me about your dreams. Do you mind?"

Pondering Evan's question, Chris gazed out at the

waves. "When I was very young, I would make up stories. You know, all about what a different life I would have one day, with a family, a real family that wanted me." All kinds of memories bubbled up inside, and she heard her voice wobble a bit at those last few words. She closed her eyes. "Can I change my mind? I guess I don't really want to talk about this."

He moved closer, his masculine presence both a comfort and a distraction, and massaged the back of her neck with sure, firm fingers. "You've had it pretty rough."

Shrugging, she said, "Rougher than some, not as rough as others." Opening her eyes, she favored him with another smile. "I imagine you have quite a story too. One of these days I'd like to hear it."

"One of these days."

"But not now?"

"Yeah, not now," he said, which wasn't much of a surprise to Chris. He was the classic strong, silent type. Not the kind of man that found talking about himself an easy thing to do.

A sea gull flew low, then swooped up into the blue sky once again. Chris watched its movements, then gazed again at the distant sailboats. "Rough or no," she said thoughtfully, "I'm grateful that it's all turned out okay. I have an education, two terrific kids, food and shelter, and the occasional laugh."

"What about passion?"

She went still for a moment. "It hasn't been an option for a while."

"I'd like to make it an option."

The hand near her shoulder stroked the side of her

neck, then cupped her chin, turning her face toward him. Chris studied him and after a while said, "I would too."

"Then what's the problem?"

"My head keeps stopping me."

"Do you always think everything over before you act?"

"Only when it concerns my kids."

He looked to his left, then to his right, then gave her a slow, simmering smile. "I don't see them anywhere," he whispered, capturing her mouth with his.

His kiss was as soft, as sure, as knowing as she remembered it. It started out gently, but intensified immediately when she felt his tongue push past her lips, its tip stroking the roof of her mouth, the soft skin inside her cheeks, then meeting her tongue and engaging in a slick, assertive dance of seduction. With a cry she opened to him.

As if there had ever been a choice.

He pulled her legs across his lap, and she felt the shape of his manhood on the backs of her knees. Oh, my, she thought, how quickly each of them got aroused when they were together. Her arm went around his neck and he angled her body toward his, effectively protecting most of their activity from any prying eyes. He rubbed a thumb up against a nipple, and through the thin material of her dress and new lingerie, Chris felt it spring to life with throbbing suddenness, puckering into a hard, tight bud. Her body had been starved for so long, she could feel her blood, her nerves, all of her juices heating up at the same time.

"Silk," he murmured. "You should always wear silk."

A voice of caution somewhere inside advised her to

slow down, that they were in public, for heaven's sake, and it was all going too fast. But the voice was drowned out by the whirl of sensations shooting through her body like a rocket. She had to touch him, and she did, reaching up under his sweater, feeling the fine, clean lines of his pectorals, the wiry curls at the center, the ridges of muscle below. Her palms skimmed his smooth skin, and the tough, small buds of his nipples.

Groaning, he planted kisses all over her face, down the side of her cheek, on her neck. His mouth found her ear and licked all the surfaces, all the while murmuring words of what he wanted to do to her, with her. She shivered as his hand stroked her arms and breasts and rib cage, his touch leaving fire wherever it landed, till he smoothed his palm over one hip and around to her buttocks.

"What's this?" he said. "What do you have on underneath?"

"Nothing." Chris felt her face reddening.

"Oh, lady," he said, his breath warm in her ear. "I wish to hell we weren't in public and in broad daylight, because then I would show you how much I appreciate that fact."

Chris came screeching back to reality and put her hand over Evan's. "But we are in public. I . . . think we'd better stop."

"Damn." He pulled away from her, raking his fingers through his hair. "How do you feel about the backseat of a car?" he said with a crooked smile.

"Not real enthusiastic." She altered her position so that once again she was sitting upright on the bench, smoothing wrinkles from her dress. "In fact, I don't think we should pursue this at all."

"You're kidding."

"I'm afraid not. Believe me, it's better this way."

"Better for who?" His nostrils flared with impatience. "Or should I say whom?"

Chris bit her bottom lip. "You're angry."

After a few moments of silence he shook his head. "No, I'm not angry, just a little . . . frustrated. I've wanted you for—"

He didn't finish his sentence; instead, he held her chin in his hand so that she couldn't avoid his intense gaze. She had to fight the urge to melt into those astonishing eyes of his, and lose all sense of herself.

"Tell me, please," he said firmly. "What is it?"

"I'm afraid."

"Of me?"

"Of me. I've done things, seen things . . ." She let the thought trail off as she continued to search his face for something, although she wasn't quite sure what.

"What kind of things?" He lowered his hand to find one of hers, curled tightly in her lap. He enveloped it in his, a gesture that was reassuring and insistent at the same time. "Tell me, Chris."

She studied their joined hands. "Things I've never talked about, not to anyone. I'm afraid if we become . . . intimate, you'll find out somehow." She raised her gaze to meet his once again. "And I'm afraid the whole thing will turn up on national television. I mean, that *is* why we met. That *is* your job, isn't it?"

Evan had no quick, glib response to that one because

she was right, dammit. He'd been hired to write her story, not to make love with her. Get a grip, he told himself. Cool down. You're acting like some randy teenager. Listen to the lady; do your job and forget about taking her to bed.

Besides, if he and Chris began an affair, well, after a while it wouldn't work. She was the kind of woman you made promises to, and he couldn't make any promises. He had nothing to give her. *Nada.*

He managed a rueful smile. "So much for Plan A. Ready for Plan B? We go to my place."

"You must be kidding."

He had to chuckle at the surprise, then downright distrust on her face. "I think we'll be able to work better there than at Marla's office. And I do mean *work*. I'll keep my hands to myself. All right with you?"

She thought about it for another moment before she nodded. "Okay. Lead the way."

The stretch of highway running parallel to the ocean eventually became much more rural and less populated. Soon Evan turned onto a dirt road that headed into the mountains. Up and up they climbed, the view of the Pacific still visible in the side mirror. And then it was out of sight as they rounded another curve, and suddenly they were on a large, flat plateau stretching to the edge of a mountain. A house stood at the far end, a sprawling one-story hacienda, white with a red tile roof. On one side of the house was a low stucco wall, on the other a corral and a barn. Beyond the property was a magnificent view of more mountains and blue sky.

As Evan pulled into the gravelled driveway and turned off the motor, a black Labrador retriever came tearing around the corner, barking joyously.

"Be right with you, Buster. Put a lid on it," he told the dog. With one arm resting over the back of Chris's seat, Evan stared straight ahead at his home. "Well, here we are. Casa Stone."

The look of pride on his face made Chris smile. "It's your haven, isn't it?" she said. "A place to go when the world gets too crazy."

He nodded. "Yeah, you got it. Come on, I think Buster wants to be introduced."

The dog was furiously wagging its tail as Chris slipped on her heels, and stuffed her panty hose in her purse. When she got out of the car, she could see the gray around the Lab's snout and the extra weight he carried around his haunches. "Buster's not a puppy, is he?" she said, offering her hand for the animal to sniff.

"Hardly. I've had him for twelve years. And I hope he'll stick around another twelve."

She hunkered down and gazed into the dog's eyes. "Hi, there," she said softly, rubbing behind the ears. "How's it going, old sport?"

Evan's heart gave a little lurch. The sight of the two of them together, making friends with each other, moved him in a curious, unfamiliar way. A woman, a dog, a home. A simple, strangely gratifying equation.

"Come on, Buster," he said. "Let's show Chris around."

The decor of Evan's home was about as masculine as Chris had ever seen, but then, Evan was about as masculine a man as she'd ever met, so it figured. Since their kiss on the beach, she'd been trying to maintain a friendly yet impersonal attitude toward the man, but oh, it was difficult, especially when he seemed to radiate heat with every movement of his body, every word from his sexy mouth.

She forced herself to concentrate on the house. The floor plan was spacious, the furnishings as comfortable and unpretentious as the land surrounding it. The walls were panelled in pine and the couches and chairs were made of large, rough-hewn wooden frames with thick cushions in Native American prints.

As she passed by one of the chairs, she ran the palm of her hand along the broad wooden arm.

"Watch out for splinters," Evan warned.

"This is hand-made, isn't it?"

"Most definitely. An early effort."

"By you? It's nice."

He shrugged nonchalantly, but she knew he was pleased. "It's one of the ways I unwind. I have a little workshop in the back of the barn. Want to see the rest?"

He showed her a large, well-equipped kitchen, a small office-den, and a couple of guest rooms. At the back of the house was the master bedroom and, pausing at the entrance, he gave a mock bow. "Care to see my lair, my dear?" he said with one raised eyebrow.

She matched his light mood with a brief curtsy. "Lead on, kind sir."

The room was wonderful—dark hardwood floors with

a few rugs scattered about. She couldn't seem to help the embarrassingly salacious images that came to mind as she stared at Evan's huge four-poster with its antique quilt throw, and looking sturdy enough to withstand an extraordinary amount of activity.

On the opposite wall was an entertainment center, and she walked over to inspect the large-screen TV, VCR, and compact disc player that were housed in the old pine armoire. His music collection consisted of Beethoven and Mahler, some Hank Williams, several operas, and Billie Holiday.

"Something for every mood," she said, running her finger along a long row of plastic CD holders. "I had no idea you liked music this much. Oh, and look!"

On the lower shelves were the videotapes, and Chris squatted down to read off the names. "Evan," she said happily. "You have *Two for the Road* . . . and *Mildred Pierce*. And oh, look, *Dark Victory*! Audrey Hepburn and Joan Crawford and Bette Davis. What more could a person want?"

"Sharon Stone and Bridget Fonda?" he said behind her.

"Newcomers," she scoffed.

"The action films are on the next shelf down."

She glanced over her shoulder. He was leaning against one of the bedposts, his arms crossed easily over his chest, a look of amusement on his face.

"Nah," she said with a grin. "I prefer romances."

The expression on his face changed subtly, less mirthful and more intense, and the previously playful mood in the room shifted with it. "So do I," he returned, his voice soft.

Awareness settled in for both of them. They were there, in Evan's bedroom, alone. And it was no accident that they were.

Chris's smile faded. Somehow she couldn't seem to stop her gaze from shifting away from his and wandering downward, past his strong nose with its slightly flaring nostrils, to his full, sensual mouth. Farther on were the taut muscles of his forearms, the casual drape of his sweater over his hips, and the way the faded fabric of his jeans curved lovingly over the rounded bulge at the juncture of his thighs.

Chris grabbed one of the shelves to keep her balance, and forced herself to look away from him. She was dizzy from the electric charge zipping along her nerve endings. Coming with him to his house was probably not a smart move on her part.

She pulled herself up and walked to the adjacent wall that was nothing but glass doors, avoiding Evan's gaze, which felt as though it were piercing her with fire. On the other side of the glass wall she saw a long oval pool, its water a much darker hue than the usual light blue she associated with Southern California pools.

Her throat felt dry, but she managed to say, "How does it get to be that color?"

Evan ambled over to her and stood behind her; she could almost sense his body heat burning into her shoulder blades. "I had it designed that way," he answered in his deep, slow drawl. "The tiles are dark green, and the water takes on that color. It looks more like the ocean than a pool, don't you think?"

What she actually thought was how could one man, dispensing information about a swimming pool, sound like he was engaging in foreplay?

"Do you use it a lot?" she asked, and her voice croaked. She saw his reflection in the window move closer to hers, and his mouth curve up at the ends. Suddenly, the act of taking in enough air became more difficult.

"When I'm on a project, if I've been writing all day, yeah. At night after dark is the best time. You can't believe how great it feels to swim in the moonlight. No suit, of course," he added with another small smile.

Their gazes met in the glass before them. "Of course," she whispered breathlessly.

He didn't touch her, but she had the memory of their fevered kiss on the beach, and she felt as though he were stroking every part of her. "It feels incredible," he said softly into her ear. "The cold water against my skin, the breeze on my face. And the sounds—crickets, birds, sometimes a coyote. Once in a while a deer comes up to the pool to have a drink and I try to stay very quiet. Usually, it's Buster who scares it away."

"This whole place is wonderful. I had no idea . . ."

She wanted to lean back and rest her head against his broad chest, wanted to close her eyes and feel his hands all over her. She bit back a nervous laugh at the direction of her thoughts. But as their eyes met in the window, she knew he was thinking the same thing. Still, he was keeping his promise. Hands off, he'd said.

It was up to her to send a signal if anything was to happen. And with all this heat between them, was it even possible for her and Evan to work together without scratching their incredible itches first?

Well, why not? Chris asked herself silently. She was a big girl. For two weeks she'd been dreaming of Evan, his hands, his mouth, fantasizing about the intoxicating pleasure of his touch. And now, here she was, alone with him on a hilltop in California. Without her kids, or Dora, or the small town filled with gossips watching their every move. Also without underwear, she added ruefully.

Could she handle an affair—more probably a brief fling, given the kind of man Evan was. Would her heart get broken? And even more important, was it possible to be intimate with Evan without revealing things it was better not to reveal? She needed time, so instead of leaning back, she took a step forward and unlatched one of the sliding glass doors.

The fresh air was almost enough to break the spell. Almost. Crossing her arms under her breasts, Chris strolled along the perimeter of the pool until she was gazing out toward the mountains. "It's a wonderful house. And you have horses, don't you?" She turned to face him. "Maybe you could show me some more of your property."

He was leaning against the open door, one bent elbow propped against the frame, and looked sexier than any man had a right to. He seemed to be studying her, assessing her mood. Then he shrugged. "Sure. How about if we eat first? I have pizza in the refrigerator."

Oh, good, she thought. Activity. "Let me help."

"No. Grab a chair," he said, pointing to a group of upholstered lounge chairs near the pool. "Put your feet up, rest a while. I won't be long."

He started to go inside, then turned to face her again. "Make sure you're here when I come back."

EIGHT

Evan walked over to the lounge where Chris lay and gazed down at her. Her pale hair covered part of her cheek, a few strands glinting in the sun. She seemed peaceful as she slept, curled up on her side, her cheek resting on a bent forearm. His heart turned over in his chest.

What was it about her? he asked himself. An emotional barrier that he always kept firmly in place was in danger of being breached by this woman, and he wasn't sure if that was a good thing. He'd kept his walls with success for all these years, but something about Chris tugged at him, reaching down under all the layers of dissipation and disappointment, and unrealized dreams, to make contact with the part of him he hadn't heard from in years, the part of him that still had some hope.

He sat down on the edge of the lounge, feeling his throat tighten as he gazed at her, experiencing a strange, sad longing for this woman. He tried to shake off the feeling. He told himself it was all about taking Chris to bed, that if the two of them could just take care of this physical attraction, he would stop all these fantasies.

Yeah, that was all it was, he assured himself—he wanted her, real bad. Wanted to bury himself in all that spirit and energy and unconscious sensuality. Bury himself to the hilt and lose all sense of who he was and where he came from.

He pushed back an errant lock of her hair, twisting it behind her ear. She swatted at his hand in her sleep, then mumbled something. Her eyes flickered open, and she favored him with a small, sleepy smile.

"I dozed off. How long have I been sleeping?"

"About fifteen minutes. Chilly?"

She shook her head. "No."

"I was wrong about the pizza," he said, pushing back another strand of hair that was about to fall over her eyelashes. "I must have eaten it the other day."

"What a shame."

Chris hadn't meant to fall asleep, but Evan's suggestion of lying down on the chaise and basking in what was left of the day's sun, of just resting for a little while and not dealing with the need to keep secrets or the way her body hummed around Evan, well, it had all sounded so good that she couldn't resist. She'd stretched out, fallen asleep, and woken up to find Evan perched on the edge of her lounge. Something in the way he looked at her made her insides melt. He might have been talking about pizza, but his gaze radiated liquid heat—and something softer. Vulnerability? Yes. And maybe a little anger at himself for feeling it. He was such a complicated man. But most definitely, no doubt about it, a man.

"We could go out to eat if you'd like," he said. "Or send out for something. Or . . ." He let the thought trail off.

"Or what?"

"Or wait till later."

Even with her mind fuzzy from sleep, Chris picked up on the nuances of that one, especially with the way he was looking at her and the husky, sexy inflection of his words. It was not about when they would dine. She told herself to take a moment to think, but before she could, the words slipped out. "I vote for later."

So much for taking a moment. So much for thinking at all.

Evan expelled a long breath. "Damn, I'm glad you said that."

Something about all the feeling he put into that sentence sent a surge of confidence through her. Woman power—to entice, to make a man sigh with wanting her— it felt wonderful. She shifted her position so that she was lying on her back and gazed up at him. The decision had been made, the signal given. What would happen now? Would he pounce or seduce slowly? She stretched her arms over her head, intending the gesture to be as provocative as it appeared. She could see her own feelings of desire reflected in the way Evan drew in a breath and narrowed his gaze.

She reached up and stroked his cheek, acutely sensitive to the stubble of his beard against her palm. "Evan?"

"I love the way you say my name." He brought her

hand to his mouth and proceeded to kiss each finger one by one. He took his time, letting his tongue stroke her skin from the pad to the fingertip, then the valleys between. And all the time he kept his gaze pinned to hers, sending messages of startling sensuality, and she felt her skin tighten with arousal.

Slow, she thought. It would be slow. And she wondered if she would please him.

Evan unfastened the button at her wrist and pushed up her sleeve, and Chris let out a deep, shuddering sigh as he transferred his kisses to the soft, creamy skin of her arm, the inside of her elbow. His tongue teased the crease there, tickling then laving it with moisture. Sensations pulsated along through her, reaching deep down into her woman's core.

"Oh, my," she said, her breathy whisper barely audible in the fading light of day. "I . . . can't . . ."

"You can't what?" Now his tongue was doing its magic on the skin farther up her arm, accompanied by small bites of the flesh that didn't hurt but somehow made her want to moan. Why hadn't she known how incredibly sensitive she was there?

She closed her eyes as the responses caused by his mouth and teeth and fingers rippled through her. "I . . . can't . . . remember anything. Where are we?"

"At my house. On a mountain. On the top of the world."

"Oh, yes, that's right."

He gently lowered the arm he'd been kissing and performed the same service for the other. Her sighs were getting louder, but she barely noticed. She was inhabiting a world of colors and feelings and wonderfully lusty sensations.

When she felt Evan shift his attention to the buttons at the front of her dress, she opened her eyes so she could watch his hands. His long, callused, sun-browned fingers brought magic with every movement. He kissed the pulse at her neck, then pulled open a button, stroking then kissing the bare skin he uncovered. He unfastened more, kissing her chest area, then moving his fingertips and lips across the soft mounds above her bra line. Another button, and a swipe of his tongue over the silk that covered her breasts, then the skin right under the front snap of her bra, and the flesh below that.

Breathing became more and more difficult with each slow, sensual movement of his mouth. He was affected too, she could tell, despite the astonishing control he was exhibiting. She felt his pulse accelerate, heard his breath coming faster with each kiss.

"I can't make up my mind," she said.

"About what?"

"If I should just lie here like some spoiled cat . . . and let you do all these wonderful things to me, or— Oh." She gasped as he flicked his tongue over one silk-encased nipple, then the other.

"Or what?"

"Or if I should be more of an . . . active participant."

"Plenty of time for both."

He teased the stiff points of her breasts with his teeth, then licked around them and over them, leaving large wet areas on her bra. The outside air hit the moistened fabric, making her nipples even more taut. The sensation now was sharp, almost painful. He sucked her through the material, and a sweet, tight, tension formed between her legs.

She groaned. "Do you have any idea what you're doing to me?"

"It's nothing compared to what I intend to do."

"I'm not sure I'll survive"— Lord, could her heart beat any faster, her breathing get any heavier—"but what a way to go."

His soft chuckle accompanied the parting of the hooks of her bra. He bent over and eased the elastic of her slip aside so his tongue could scour her belly button. She lifted her hips to help him remove the slip. Then the bra. In the next moment Chris was naked, and she shivered.

Evan drew her up to a sitting position and enveloped her in a hug. "You're cold," he said, his mouth against her neck. "I'm sorry. I just wanted to see you."

"No, I'm not cold, just a little—" She didn't finish her sentence, but wrapped her arms around his broad back and held tight.

"A little what?"

"Oh, Evan, something about you makes me feel . . . giddy, awkward. It's like it's the first time."

He drew his head back and met her gaze with an expression that was warm and sensual. "It is," he whispered as his eyes swept over her body. "And you—all of you—are as beautiful as I imagined you would be."

She barely had time to savor the pleasure of his words

before he drew her closer and his mouth descended on hers.

There was so much hunger in the way his lips met hers that Chris was startled. But only for a moment. Then she threw away all remaining hesitancy and returned his kiss with an urgency that matched his. The slow part was over. All the yearning they had been feeling toward each other for what seemed like an eternity was unleashed in that kiss.

He plunged his tongue between her lips and she met it eagerly with her own, invading his mouth even as she welcomed him to hers. Rough, then tender, soft, and wet, their lips clung while their tongues explored every part of each other's mouths. It was as though they needed to possess every part of the other.

Evan was the one who broke the kiss, and Chris groaned.

"Just a moment," he whispered. "I'm overdressed."

Then he stood. He was impossibly tall and masculine, and she watched avidly as he removed his sweater. Her heart sped up at the sight of his bare chest, all muscles and hard planes, and she emitted a small, involuntary sigh.

His smile at her appreciation was slightly self-mocking but confident at the same time. "I pass inspection, do I?"

"Most definitely."

"Shall I remove the rest?"

"Yes, please. And quickly."

He chuckled and discarded his boots and jeans, and finally his briefs. None of her fantasies had even come close to Evan as he stood before her. Sun-browned skin and ridges of muscle and sinew, wiry curls on his chest and another thatch between his sturdy, long legs, out of which jutted the hard, thick evidence of his arousal.

Her mouth suddenly went dry, and she licked her lips. Evan's nostrils flared, and a look of intense heat replaced his amusement. He leaned over her, taking her by surprise as he scooped her up into his arms. "How do you feel about swimming?"

"Swimming?"

"Yep."

She clung to his neck as he walked over to the shallow edge of the pool, then stepped down onto the first step. "You sure about this?" she said, her grip on him tightening.

"You do know how to swim, don't you?"

"Sure, but I thought we were . . . well, engaging in a somewhat different form of recreation."

He smiled. "We are."

She kept her arms around his neck as they descended, and she blessed him for his foresight as he lowered them both into the pool. The water was heavenly, like a warm, soothing bath, and only made the sexual urgency she'd been experiencing with Evan more languid, not as sharp. When all but their heads were covered by water, Evan remained standing while Chris, still holding on to him, let her body float back and forth with the gentle waves generated by their movements.

He kissed her again, his tongue devouring her. She ran her fingers through his hair while he supported her with one arm and used his other hand to caress the rest of her. She sighed, unable to remember ever being treated like this, as though she were cherished, as though she were the center of someone's universe. This was total bliss, she thought, kissing Evan and feeling his hands on her shoulders, her breasts, smoothing down her hips to her ankles, and up her legs to the top of her thighs.

And finally his hand reached the thatch of hair at the intersection of her thighs, and his fingers touched the tight, throbbing center of sensation nestled among the folds there. Using the pad of his thumb, he lavished the same attention on the small hard nub as he had on the rest of her, and soon she lost the sense of everything else except the heat between her and Evan, and the waves of pleasure coursing through her body.

"Evan," she moaned, unable to stay still, rotating her hips, curling into him for more. "Oh, Evan. That feels—" She was breathing too hard to finish her sentence.

She cried out again at the slow, tantalizing, insistent pressure of his caress. She drank it in, felt the air on her skin. Behind her closed eyelids she sensed the ripples of illumination and shadow caused by the late afternoon sunlight and heard the slap of the water against the tiles on the side of the pool.

The muscles of her body contracted even more, and an almost unbearable pressure began to build, radiating from that single point at her core. "Evan, what are you doing?"

Her back arched, she felt her hair floating all around her. He continued to stroke between her legs even as he licked one hardened nipple. "Giving you what you deserve. Pleasure."

"But—"

"But what?" He licked the other nipple, his tongue's movement matching the rhythm of his finger.

She thought she might lose her mind. "I want to give you pleasure too."

"Oh, lady," he groaned. "That's what you're doing."

He increased the pressure of his assault on her senses, his stroking fingers, his tongue moving more rapidly and more firmly. She felt herself pulsating with his movements, heard her loud moans echoing in her ears. The tide of her excitement rose to a higher, more fevered pitch, until she found herself on the edge of what she could stand, then past the edge and into the abyss.

Stars exploded, one after the other after the other. Her body spasmed, sending larger waves throughout the pool, and all the while Evan held her tightly, his fingers, his tongue never stopping till she screamed her release into the fading day.

She slumped against him, drained of all energy, knowing that she had just come apart, but that Evan would support her, hold her, put her back together again. She curled into his body and felt his gentle kisses along her neck.

Holding on to his shoulders, Chris let her legs drift down until her body was aligned with his. She couldn't miss the hard ridge of his erection against her thighs. Reaching between their bodies, she curled her fingers around him.

He groaned and kissed her mouth. Then he broke the kiss, and eased her hand away, saying, "No. Wait."

"Why?" She reached for him again, but he was too quick for her. He picked her up and carried her out of the pool.

"You keep carrying me places," she said.

"You got it."

After grabbing several thick towels from the cabana nearby, he eased open the sliding glass doors to his bedroom.

"I know this is hopelessly middle class of me," he said, "but would you care to try my bed?"

"I thought you'd never ask."

They laughed and fell onto the bed, rubbing each other all over with the towels. Evan reached into his side drawer for a condom, and Chris rested her head on his ribs. "That was why you told me to wait. Thank you. I really appreciate it."

"And I really appreciate you. In so many ways."

"Oh, Evan," she said, reaching for him. "This whole day has been magic."

"The day's not over yet."

He moved his body over hers, and it was Chris's turn to get her fill of touching him, up and down and over the hard male planes of him, the ridges of muscle, the tough, springy hair that rasped enticingly against her skin. He smelled of chlorine and sex, and she felt dizzy from his presence.

She reached between their bodies to cup him again. "Now?"

"Now."

Groaning Chris's name, Evan plunged into her with a quick, shocking thrust that took his breath away. She wrapped her legs around his waist, her arms around his neck, and he could hardly contain his excitement. God, she felt amazing, but he wanted even more. Placing his hands under her buttocks, he pulled her hips even tighter to his, and then he was so deep inside her, he wondered if he'd ever find his way back, or would even want to.

It had never been like this with any other woman, not once. He lost time and place, he lost his isolation and loneliness, even the hard, brittle edges of his soul. Chris was here—finally!—in his bed and in his arms.

When he woke a short time later, the room was in shadows. He reached for Chris, who was supposed to be next to him in his bed. But she wasn't.

Disoriented, Evan looked around the room, then through the glass door. In the far corner of the pool area she sat on a chaise lounge, curled up in his old terry-cloth robe, gazing into the distance.

He felt a small dart of worry at the look on her face—thoughtful, and way too sad. He pulled on his jeans and sweater, slipped his feet into a pair of moccasins, then went out to her. "Hey," he said, lowering himself onto the chaise. "Why are you out here when I'm in there?"

She gazed at him without smiling. "My head is jabbering at me."

"What's it saying?"

"Told you so, told you so."

He studied her for a couple of moments, feeling his

old, familiar self-protectiveness shifting into place. "I take it you're having regrets," he said stiffly.

She put her hand on his and smiled wistfully. "Not regrets. It was too beautiful for regrets."

"What then?" he asked, his tension abating slightly.

"I let myself forget why we're here. We're supposed to be working on the script, and I'm supposed to tell you all kinds of things about me. And now that we've . . . made love"—she shrugged—"I don't have any defenses. Defenses I'm pretty sure I'm going to need."

He studied her for a moment longer, then rose from the chaise and gave her his hand. "Come."

"Where to?"

"A place not far from here, to watch the sun set. We can walk."

"But all I have is my heels."

"True. Wait right there."

He returned to his room and found some thick socks for her. Then he went back to the pool, sat down, and put them on her feet. "I usually dress myself," she said.

"Indulge me." He scooped her up into his arms.

He liked carrying Chris. Maybe it was one of those caveman-claiming-his-woman things, but hell, he was allowed. He went around to the side of the house and eased open a small wrought iron gate. Pushing back a couple of overhanging tree branches, he made his way up the hill.

She snuggled into his chest, her arms around his neck. "I suppose I should protest at how much you've been manhandling me."

"Protest away."

"I don't feel like it."

"Good."

It was cool and quiet—and private—up here, which was why he lived on the mountain. Autumn was his favorite season. The leaves were turning; the air was a little nippy as evening approached. All around there was the smell of damp earth and dying leaves. Buster appeared to keep them company, barking at various flying insects, and chasing a sea gull.

"Go get 'im, Buster," Evan said.

Chris raised her head from his shoulder. "I must be heavy."

"Shoot, little lady, you're a feather."

She laughed, then her eyes narrowed with speculation. "I can't place your accent, Evan."

"I don't have an accent."

"Of course you don't," she said. "But if you did, where would it be from?"

"I'm a Wyoming boy, born and bred."

"I thought it was something like that," she said, nodding and resting her head on his shoulder again. "You fairly reek of the Old West."

"I'll remember to wear deodorant next time."

"That was awful," she said with a groan. "Are you sure you're a professional writer?"

"Madam," he said, "you have cut me to the quick."

Her laughter was muffled by her hand and he thought she looked about four years old. He gave her a quick kiss on the mouth, relieved that her mood had lightened. Time enough to be serious later.

"Here we are." He carried her past a group of tall pine trees to a clearing at the edge of a cliff. Once there, he set her down. Draping one arm over her shoulder, he pointed. "Here's what I brought you to see."

Stretching out before them was a magnificent view of the ocean far below—gray and blue and vast as it blended into the darkening skyline. Traffic streamed along the highway, but the cars and trucks seemed like toys. By then the sun was almost obliterated by the horizon, and the clouds took on a darker hue, streaking across the sky.

"Oh, Evan, it's wonderful."

"Yeah," he said, feeling absurdly pleased with her reaction, as though he had somehow personally engineered the beauty in front of them.

"The sky," she said. "Those colors. It's an amazing display."

"It's the smog. Something about the carbon dioxide mixing in with the haze and the dirt that makes it look like that."

She angled her head around. "So much for illusion."

He shrugged. "Knowing what causes something doesn't make it any less beautiful."

"I suppose not. Is there anything you're sentimental about?"

He thought about it for a moment. Two images came to mind—the mental snapshot he'd taken earlier in the day of Chris and Buster in front of his home. And Chris lying on the chaise, asleep, before they made love. "Not really," he said.

"That's what I figured."

He walked over to the base of one of the tall trees and sat down, leaning back against the trunk. Patting a bed of pine needles next to him, he said, "Come sit and watch the sun set."

She walked over to the tree and lowered herself onto the ground next to him. She drew her knees up to her chest and put her arms around them, staring out at the ribbons of pink and gray streaking across a darkening sky. Neither of them spoke for a while, and he massaged the back of her neck, wanting to ease her fears.

"There's something pretty heavy in your past, isn't there?" he said. "Have you done time in jail? Is that it?"

Her soft laugh was humorless. "No, I haven't spent time in jail, not a real jail anyway. I was locked up in a juvenile facility for a while."

"What for?"

Chris turned and studied Evan's face before she replied. The moment was terribly important; they'd made love, shared the most intimate physical act possible, and yet he was still a stranger in so many ways. He sat inches from her, an expression of intense concentration on his face. He was such a large presence. Broad. Sensual. Masculine. Unforgettable.

The night was further advanced now. A pale half-moon was visible, and the light continued to fade. Everything was stillness and shadows, and Chris felt her destiny was hanging in the air around them.

"How much can I tell you," she said, "and know it will go no further?"

NINE

She exchanged a thoughtful look with Evan for what seemed like a long time. Finally, he spoke. "Do you trust me?"

After another several moments she answered, "Actually, I do. Although I'm not sure why."

His mouth quirked up at one corner. "A backhanded compliment if ever I've heard one."

"I didn't mean—"

He waved away her protest. "It's all right."

His expression turned serious once again. The turquoise of his eyes was more silver in the waning light, but no less riveting as they looked deeply into hers. "Then here's what I want you to know. I may not have a lot of principles left, but when I say something, I mean it. And I'm saying this: Nothing you tell me will turn up on national television unless you want it to. Nothing."

"But Marla said—" Chris shook her head.

"What did Marla say?"

"That she knows some of . . . my secrets. Well, she hinted she did anyway. That's why I agreed to come. I mean, I didn't want my name and my story showing up as some item in a gossip column."

"Did you get yourself a lawyer? Someone to protect your interests?"

"No. I probably should have, but—" She shrugged. "I wanted to keep the whole thing low-key and uncomplicated. I just wanted it to be over."

"But Marla played hard ball."

"You did warn me."

"Yeah, I warned you."

Evan picked up a handful of pine needles and sifted them slowly through his fingers, as though contemplating several options. Then his eyes met hers again. "It'll all work out, I promise. Talk to me, Chris. Please."

She expelled a breath. "I guess I'm going to have to."

"Are you cold? Do you want to head back to the house?"

"Not just yet," she said, pulling his robe tighter to her. "I love it up here."

"I knew you would."

Sitting back against the tree trunk, he pulled her into the cradle of his bent legs. She propped her arms on his knees and leaned back against his chest. It was time, and they both knew it.

"Tell me, Chris," he said. "Tell me all of it."

Looking out at the night, she began. She told him about the foster homes, one after the other, and how she kept forgetting the names of each new set of parents and siblings until she finally stopped trying. About how she was on the streets at thirteen, part of a gang; at fifteen she'd been caught stealing and was locked up. She was released a few months later and that same day, near the Greyhound Bus terminal, she was approached.

"Recruited, really," Chris told Evan, "by a kid about my age with a shaved head. He told me all about myself, about my anger and my need to be part of a family, that he'd been there and really understood. And he said he would show me a place where I would be safe and loved and taken care of. It sounded too good to be true, but oh, how I wanted to believe him. I wound up in Arizona at the Vargas Ranch, near Sedona. It was the home of a cult, as it turned out. The Chelsea Gang."

"The Chelsea Gang," Evan said. "I remember reading about them."

"Then you know their leader was Edward Chelsea and he was an amazing man. Brilliant. Filled with a kind of magical charm."

As she spoke, Chris pictured Edward's face and the way he had used his eyes and his hands and a sort of fevered poetry to weave intricate webs around all of them. She shuddered at the memory.

"Apparently, he'd started out as a fairly normal person, but by the time I met him he'd been driven insane from years of taking all kinds of hallucinogens. But I didn't know that, not at first. I was sixteen. I fell desperately in love with him, what I thought was love, a kind of lover-father-brother thing, I guess."

She clutched at Evan's knees for a moment. "I was so starved for affection, so needy. I was ripe for the picking."

"Yeah, that's the kind of kid those groups get their hooks into."

If his words were neutral, the way he was touching her was far from it. His hands had been resting lightly on her shoulders. Now he increased the pressure of his touch, and Chris understood that he was feeling for her, and was angry at the people who long ago had taken advantage of her youth, and susceptible state of mind.

"Anyway, I shaved my head, and studied Scripture, Edward's version, of course. And after an elaborate ceremony, I became one of his 'sacred wives.' There were ten of us—a harem, really—but I was so proud to be one of ten. To be needed, to be special.

"I'd been there over a year—almost two, I think. It was a couple of months before my eighteenth birthday— when I found I was pregnant." She paused, then went on. "With Brian."

"I see."

"I'd begun to realize that I'd made a mistake, but I wasn't quite sure what to do about it. I had no family, no one to turn to. I tried to leave, but they hauled me back, saying that the child I was carrying was one of the Chosen, and I had to stay and nurture him and prepare him. I wasn't quite sure what I was to prepare him for, but I'd seen and heard a lot of very . . . disturbing things since I'd been there—" She stopped for a moment and closed her eyes as shocking, distasteful pictures flashed in her brain, pictures she hadn't allowed herself to remember in a very long time.

Evan must have felt the added tension in her body, because he said, "Hey, Chris, you all right?"

She reached for his hand and he entwined their fingers. "Yes," she said. "I'll tell you more about that year some other time. All you need to know is that I was scared to death. I knew that if I didn't do something radical, I would be in big trouble.

"I tried to escape one more time, and this time they locked me in a room. After about a month I started to go a little crazy. They fed me, but all I had was a bed, the holy books they gave me, and a few square feet to pace around. I thought I'd never get through it; I thought I might lose my mind."

"God, Chris," he said.

She nodded. "Yeah, it was pretty rough. But—" She sighed. "Fate intervened. The neighbors had been complaining for a while and got up some sort of vigilante committee to investigate. One of Edward's men started shooting, and suddenly there were gunshots all around. I heard screaming and crying." She shuddered, but the reassuring pressure of Evan's hand gave her the strength she needed to continue on. "A bullet whizzed through the window, missing me by about an inch. I managed to get the window open and ran for my life. I found myself on the highway in the middle of the night with nothing. No money, no clothing except a thin skirt and T-shirt. It was summer, so I didn't freeze, at least. I was about four months pregnant."

"Thank God you got away."

"Yes, I know. And I can't believe how lucky I was then. I made my way to a truck stop and started talking to a young woman I met there. She was about my age— Tory, her name was. She was a student at the University of Colorado at Boulder. It was summer then—I told you that, didn't I? She'd just been on a trip, working on a reservation, and was heading back to her home in Denver. She offered me a lift and I took it. I needed to get out of Arizona and I didn't care where, as long as it was far away. She asked me my name and I told her it was Christine Day. That wasn't my real name, of course."

"What is your real name?"

"You mean what name was I assigned by the state of Illinois?" She was amazed how much it still bothered her, even after all these years. "Jane Smith. Imaginative, huh? Plain Jane Smith, the kids used to say. Christine Day was a name I made up for myself in my fantasies as a kid; I thought it sounded kind of elegant and, I don't know, perky at the same time. So when Tory asked my name, I didn't even hesitate.

"And I had to wipe out my other identity. I was terrified that they'd find me, the police, the cult—whoever was left, that is. I wanted to lose myself completely. I remember how nice Tory was to me even though I think I must have looked kind of weird. I was really skinny and my head had been shaved a couple of months earlier. . . ."

Evan kissed the top of her head. "I'll bet you looked beautiful."

"Trust me, I looked weird. Anyway, traveling with Tory, talking about school and classes and stuff like that—normal things—well, it turned me around. I had always loved to read. Movies and books got me through my childhood, I think. So now I had a goal. I would have my baby, I would give it up for adoption, and I would get an education. I would make something of myself. Tory was nice enough to lend me a hundred dollars—I paid her back, by the way—and I got this waitress job in Denver, and a small room nearby."

She gazed up at the first few stars of the evening. All around were the noises of nighttime—leaves rustling, crickets, the faint cry of an animal in the distance. She breathed in the clean air and went on.

"When I had Brian, I couldn't give him up, I just couldn't. I knew that keeping him would make my life more difficult, but that's the way it was. I had some help from an elderly lady at the rooming house, and I kept working. I took the equivalency test and went to a community college for two semesters to get the grades I needed. I was so tired, Evan, so tired all the time. Brian was about eighteen months old when I started at Boulder, and spilled the eggs on John."

She paused and closed her eyes, finally allowing herself to lean all her weight against Evan's firm chest. She didn't know how much more energy she had. "The rest of the story isn't quite as dramatic."

"Just a little more. Tell me about John."

Again Chris sensed more than idle curiosity behind Evan's words. She hesitated. She wanted to tell it all, and that meant not spouting some myth that she'd been promoting for years to avoid problems.

"I never loved my husband," she said quietly. "It shamed me sometimes, but that's the truth. He was a very nice man. A good man. I told him some of what happened, but not all. He knew I'd been in trouble as a teenager and that Brian's father and I hadn't married, but

I . . . left out the part about Edward Chelsea. John offered to marry me and to adopt Brian and, well, I said I would. I never regretted it, but sometimes I got scared."

"Of what?"

She felt her shoulders stiffening as she remembered how it had been with John, the edginess that would creep into his voice, the way he would look at her as though she were a terrible puzzle to him. His discomfort with their physical intimacy, her own feelings of failure that she couldn't be what he needed her to be, no matter how she tried.

"I was young and scared when we met, and I worked hard to be a good wife to him," she said, choosing her words carefully. "But there was this . . . restlessness in me. I had all kinds of energy, and John was a quiet person, a little defeated by life, I think. He always wondered why I couldn't just settle for what was in front of me, why I always had to dream. . . ."

"You do have a pretty strong zest for life, you know. It was one of the first things I noticed about you."

"Do I? I suppose I do." She sighed and shook her head. "It was difficult for John, that I do know. But I was contented, really I was. Compared to the past, it was bliss. My father-in-law—Joseph McConnell—was one of the warmest, most loving people I'd ever met. I felt accepted for the first time in my life. My son had a father. *And* a grandfather. I was part of a family, and I'm not sure anyone but another orphan can understand what that means.

"I graduated college, went on to get a teaching credential, and had Lisa."

"Do the children know they're half brother and sister?"

"Yes. Everyone thinks I made a rash teenage marriage, and then got divorced. John told me his folks would never accept me if they thought I'd had a child out of wedlock. Before he introduced me to them he told me how conservative they were, how conservative the town was, so I went along. I wanted so much to be accepted, you see."

"Of course I do."

"It's why we still live with Dora. Now that both Joseph and John are gone, she's the only family my kids have. And it's even more important to keep the secret, especially about who my son's real father was."

She twisted her body around so she could face him. She had just enough energy left to make this point clear. "Do you see why I need to keep my past secret? Can you imagine how the good citizens of Loman would react?" she said with a rueful laugh, feeling a clutch of emotion gathering in her throat. "I don't think they would take too kindly to an ex–juvenile delinquent, ex-cultist with an illegitimate child who was living among them under an assumed name, teaching their children."

She swallowed. "The thing is, Evan, my life was a mess before I met John. I lied to him, then we lied to his folks. The whole thing has been a bunch of lies. One on top of the other. Make a movie about that."

"And what a movie it would make," Evan said, whistling softly. "From a writer's viewpoint, of course. It's a great story, very human, with an incredibly brave woman at its center."

"But it's *my* story," Chris said fiercely. "A private

journey that's no one's business but my own. If any of it gets out . . ." She wiped around her mouth with her thumb and index finger, then dropped her hand to her lap. "I really don't care about me," she added softly. "I mean that, Evan. But it could harm my children. And that can't happen."

"Yeah." Evan nodded a couple of times. "Yeah, I see."

She worried her bottom lip. "What do I do?"

"Nothing."

"Nothing?"

"Sure. Don't hassle it."

"But what about Marla?"

He took her hand in his and rubbed the pad of his thumb over her palm. "Marla has a few secrets of her own, you know, and I'm pretty skilled at playing hardball myself. You can't survive out here without it. It will all work out fine. Trust me."

She searched his face a moment longer, wanting to believe him, not knowing for sure if she could. But what choice did she have? She would trust him because the other option wasn't acceptable.

Having decided that, her body slumped involuntarily; she felt like a rag doll that had had the stuffing pulled out of it. "I'm wiped out. And starving. You haven't fed me yet."

Evan stood up, pulling her with him. "Come, let's go back to my place."

"Whatever you say."

"That's how I like my women. Pliable."

"In your dreams. I'm just too tired to think."

"I guess you'd better assume the position, then."

"Pardon?"

"I'm about to manhandle you again," he said with a crooked smile, scooping her up into his arms and heading for home.

Evan found pasta and sauce and garlic bread in his freezer, and after zapping everything in the microwave, served Chris and watched as she ate with all the enthusiasm of someone breaking a two-day fast. He put away a good-size meal himself, but he couldn't stop looking at her and thinking about all she'd told him. Her story moved him—not just the details of it, but the way she'd fought for survival at every turn, and the amount of sacrifices she'd made on the altar of "belonging" somewhere. He mulled it over as they ate, the writer in him already shaping scenes and hearing lines in his head.

After they'd cleaned up the kitchen and fallen into his bed, Chris turned on her side and smiled happily at him. "I feel wonderful, do you?"

He grunted. "What I feel is full."

"Yeah, well, in spite of the meal I just packed away, I feel like I've lost about a hundred pounds. And it was all tension and secrets. Years of them. You should hang out a shingle. Do you realize that's twice I've spilled my guts to you?"

"Yeah, I guess it is."

She reached over and stroked his cheek. "I'm talking too much, huh."

"No."

"The thing is, I still don't know what it is about you that makes me feel so safe. Got any ideas?"

Evan shook his head, wanting to feel her touch on more of his skin. "Not a one."

"People don't normally pour out their hearts to you, do they?"

"People don't normally get that close." He covered her hand with his and angled his head so he could plant a kiss on her palm, then placed it back on his cheek. "I don't let them."

"Yeah, I kind of knew that."

"I sure would like to get close to you now."

"Again?"

"Afraid so."

"Then what's stopping you?" she said in a voice that was somewhere between a smile and a sigh.

"Not a damned thing."

The shrill ringing of the phone incorporated itself into what had been a wonderful, sexy dream. Chris mumbled a protest, then sat up in bed with alarm as Evan plucked the receiver from its cradle.

"Marla?" he barked, wiping a hand over his face. "What the hell time is it?" He listened some more, then frowned. "Why? . . . Yes, she's here."

"Is there something wrong with my kids?" Chris whispered, panicked. "I should have phoned the hotel for messages last night."

He covered the receiver and said, "Nothing's wrong with the kids," then spoke into the phone again with barely suppressed impatience. "Yes, we've been working on the script . . . Cut the crap, Marla . . . Yes, I'll have a rough outline by Saturday. Very rough . . ." He frowned. "I'm not sure."

He held the receiver to his chest and gazed at Chris. "She wants to know if you're going to be here or at the hotel. I could tell her it's none of her business . . ."

Chris shook her head. "No, that wouldn't be right. After all, she *did* bring me out here, and she *is* paying for the trip."

"So, what shall I tell her?"

She searched his face for some indication of what he was feeling or wanted her to do, but his expression was unreadable. This was a different Evan from the one she'd been with yesterday. This one was distant and decidedly irritable. Suddenly, the fact that she was sitting in his bed, stark naked, didn't feel right. She pulled the sheet over her breasts and shrugged. "Tell Marla whatever you'd like."

What an awful way to wake up, she thought. Instead of basking in some wonderful morning-after memories, instead of snuggling in Evan's arms, she had to confront a man who looked as though he might regret what had happened between them. Did he regret it? Oh, Lord, had she made a monumental mistake?

Evan stared at her for a moment more, then spoke into the receiver again. "She's going to be in and out. Look, if you want her, leave word at the hotel; she'll either be there, or she'll check in for messages . . . I'll see." He covered the mouthpiece. "She wants to speak to you."

Chris shook her head vigorously and whispered, "Tell her I'm in the bathroom."

With a half-smile he spoke into the phone. "She's indisposed . . . You heard me . . ." He scowled. "God, Marla, get a life . . . Yeah . . . Okay, sure. Later."

He hung up the phone, shaking his head. "The woman has all the subtlety of an atom bomb. She sends her love. Also, she's throwing a 'little gathering,' a euphemism for a major party, on Saturday night. In your honor."

"Oh."

"You can tell her to forget it if you want."

Chris considered this new piece of information. "Can I really? I'm not sure. I have to be careful with Marla, don't I? But I didn't want any publicity."

"It's a little late to worry about publicity," he said dryly. "We're making a movie about you."

"I suppose you're right. What kind of party? I mean, who will be there?"

He shrugged indifferently. "The usual. Actors, writers, industry people."

In spite of the offhand way he said them, Evan's words caused a flutter of excitement in Chris, and she bit back a little laugh. "It sounds like it might be kind of fun. I'm not used to that kind of thing, the way you are. What do you think?"

That same closed expression was on his face again as he raised his shoulders. "Whatever."

This change, this abruptness of his, was making her feel extremely uncomfortable. Also angry and hurt. And worried. He'd told her she could trust him; now she wondered if she'd been a fool of the first order for listening to him.

"Evan, I—"

"We have some more background work we need to do on the script," he said abruptly. "We can do it at Marla's office, here, wherever you want. Do you want to go back to the hotel?"

"Well, I have all my clothes there . . ."

He nodded and hopped out of bed. "Sure. Are you hungry?" he asked, grabbing a short robe from a hook near the door and putting it on. "Why don't you take a shower and I'll scramble us up some eggs."

"Evan—"

"Bacon too, I think. I could eat the proverbial horse."

"Evan, stop! What's going on?"

He'd been on his way out the door when her question froze him in his tracks. Turning, Evan regarded Chris. She sat on the bed, clutching a sheet to her chest, and gazed at him, her gray eyes large and vulnerable and confused.

"You've shut down," she said. "Was it something I did?"

So many emotions were churning inside him that all he could do was look at her for a few moments without speaking. Then he shook his head slowly. "Nothing, you did nothing. I had this—" He raked his fingers through his hair. "I don't know. I had this plan, and then Marla screwed it up."

"What plan?"

He walked over to the bed and sat on the edge. He fidgeted with the belt of the robe and kept his voice as flat as possible. "I wanted you to spend all the time you have here. With me, at my house, until you have to leave on Sunday. But I understand that you need to go to the hotel. Maybe you even want to take a little break. From me . . ." He let his sentence trail off, aware that he was feeling too raw to go on.

Chris seemed to sense his mood, because she scooted down to where he was sitting and put her hand over his. "I kind of had a dream too."

"Yeah?"

She nodded. "That I could be a tourist, see some of the places I've been reading about for years. And that maybe you would take me—remember you said you would?—and we could talk on the way." She smiled. "Into a tape recorder if you'd like. And I do need to go to the hotel, for a change of clothes anyway. I'd like to stay there, in fact, at least part of the time. I've never been to a place like that—three telephones and little chocolates on your pillow. I kind of wanted to experience that."

"I see."

"But, Evan," she said softly, bringing her hand up and brushing some of his hair off his forehead, "in my dream you were there too. With me. The whole time."

His half-smile was chagrined. "Sounds kind of like my dream."

"You noticed."

"So I'm being a horse's ass this morning."

"Yes, I guess you are, just a bit." She brought her hand to his chest and splayed her fingers across it. "But I've found out your secret now. When your feelings are hurt, you shut down. I'll remember."

He watched her hand caress his chest. "Am I that transparent?"

"Like a squeaky-clean window." She eased the fabric of his robe off his shoulders and it fell around him onto the bed.

He pulled the rest of the garment from under him and tossed it on the floor. "Hmm. I'll have to work on that, or else I'll lose my credentials in the manly man club."

"Not a lot of danger of that."

His nipples were hard now, and he loved what her fingertips were doing to them. "Listen, Chris, I want all your time while you're here. Got that? All of it. And if that means I have to trudge out to Disneyland, well, what the hell. We'll go to Disneyland."

She flicked his nipples with her fingernails and he drew in a breath. He grabbed her hand and held it tightly to his chest.

"Can I stand in the footprints in front of Mann's Theater?" Chris asked.

"Way overrated."

She pulled her hand away playfully. "Fine, I'll go on one of those tour buses—"

"Nah, I'll take you."

Just then one of their stomachs gave a loud rumble and they looked down in the direction of their own midriffs. Then when they looked up at the same time, and their eyes met, they laughed.

"I guess I'd better see what I can rustle up in the kitchen," Evan said. He rose from the bed and bent down to retrieve his robe.

"Cowboy, you have the most amazing body," Chris said in that low, honeyed voice of hers.

He forgot about the robe and faced her. "I do?"

She leaned back on her elbows, allowing the sheet to fall away from her breasts. As she raked his body with a hungry gaze, his muscles, his skin, all of him, tensed up with desire for her.

"You're everything a man is supposed to be," she said, "and I can't believe my good luck in finding you."

She looked directly at the juncture of his thighs, and he directed his gaze to the same place. "Well, well," he said with a smile. "Good morning to you."

"Yes, it is," Chris said. "A fine morning." She fell back on the bed and, her lids lowered, stretched lazily. The movement of her arms made her creamy breasts rounder and higher. "You make me feel utterly wanton, you know."

"Gee, I had no idea . . ."

What was happening to him? he wondered as his hot stare roamed over her body. He had never been this moody, this possessive, this *emotional*, with a woman before. And he'd certainly never wanted a woman this badly, with such urgency.

"Maybe breakfast can wait a few minutes," he said, one knee on the bed as he bent over her.

She raised an eyebrow. "Minutes?"

"Minutes, hours. I'm flexible."

"Want to show me just how flexible?"

"Oh, lady, it will be my pleasure."

"And mine, most definitely," she said.

And then his mouth put a stop to all further talking.

TEN

"You were right," Chris said, walking over to Evan where he stood, arms folded over his chest, leaning against a No Parking sign. "It *is* overrated."

Evan allowed himself to look smug. "Told you."

She gestured toward the large concrete expanse in front of the Mann's Theater. "But it's also wonderful. I mean, look at all the people here, from all over the world, all different races and languages. And did you see that very large woman who was trying to fit into that tiny footprint—whose was it?" Chris scurried over, bent to read the name, then returned to him. "Myrna Loy." She sighed happily. *"The Thin Man. The Best Years of Our Lives."*

"Good ol' Myrna."

Chris put her arms around his neck. "Thanks, Evan."

Smiling down at her, he cupped her shoulders with his hands. "For what?"

"Putting up with me. I mean, I love this place. I love

all the silly red pagoda roofs, and the silly red ushers' uniforms and, I don't know, all of it."

He shook his head. "You're incredible."

"Thanks, I think."

"You can look around at all this"—he pointed to the crowded, dirty boulevard with its faded glory and the pervasive odor of gas fumes—"and see only the fantasy."

"But you see only the harshness. Why?"

He thought about it for a moment. "I don't think of it as harshness. To me it's reality."

"Is it?"

"I work here, remember?" He chuckled. "It's like asking someone to believe in the wonder and magic of Las Vegas when he's got a job in the kitchen peeling onions and emptying garbage. After you've seen what's behind the glamour, how can you take it seriously?"

Chris looked at him as though he hadn't quite answered her question, so he raked his fingers through his hair and looked off into the distance. After a while he said, "I don't know, maybe it's because I'm a writer, and writers have to stay detached."

"Detached, yes. But . . ." She didn't finish her thought. Instead, she put her arm through his and pointed to a garishly decorated café nearby. "Come on," she said. "Buy me a cup of coffee."

"Sure you can tear yourself away from Myrna?"

"I'll manage."

He put his hand over hers, and they strolled along the busy street. He couldn't remember when he'd last spent time like this—ambling about town and seeing the sights. His social life was pretty unexciting, he supposed, consisting of casual friendships with other writers, some poker buddies. The occasional short-lived affair. He couldn't take many people for too long. He was a solitary kind of man with a solitary kind of life. A life he'd thought was working pretty well.

But he'd been with Chris constantly since early afternoon the day before, and not once had he had the desire to be anywhere else but with her. Most especially not alone, without her.

That morning, after they'd eaten enough breakfast to —as Chris had laughingly observed—"fill up a bear about to go into hibernation," they'd worked awhile. He asked questions and she answered, although he could tell she was still worried about the movie, about the parts of her life that would wind up on TV, and how much privacy she'd have left when it was all over.

Hell, he didn't blame her. The media chewed up and spit out people's lives like fast food, and never gave a thought to who was being victimized. Chris would relax only when she saw the finished script; it would be a pretty good one, he thought. Her stories about the kids and Dora, about the town of Loman and teaching school there, would provide good local color. The real work, he knew, would begin when he sat at his computer after Chris returned to Loman.

After Chris returned to Loman.

He didn't care much for that thought, and as they walked along Hollywood Boulevard, he squeezed her hand a little too tightly.

"Hey," she said. "There are bones in there."

"Sorry."

He was reluctant to tell her that he didn't want her to leave. In fact, his chest ached at the thought. Oh, man, he was in trouble, and it was his own damned fault for telling Marla he'd write the script. If he hadn't set eyes on Chris again— If he hadn't taken her to bed—

But he had. And he wanted to keep her.

Where would this thing with her lead? He didn't believe in happy endings, never had. But he was feeling different somehow. After only twenty-four hours with Chris, a little bit of ice was melting somewhere inside him. Damn. He hated change.

At the coffee shop Chris smiled at the good-natured woman with frizzy blond hair and false eyelashes who showed them to their table. She reminded her of a cocktail waitress at the Loman Arms bar. Propping an elbow on the table, Chris leaned her chin on her hand and gazed out at the passersby with interest.

A man who resembled the robber at the convenience store that night hurried by, and a small rush of fear skittered through her. She wondered if, living here in a large, modern city, a person got used to all the underlying violence. Of course it didn't really matter, not to her. She didn't live there. She had a home, a family, and a job. In Loman.

After they ordered ice cream sodas, she turned her attention back to Evan. "Okay, tell me," she said, "were you always like this?"

"How am I?"

"The-glass-is-half-empty type."

Even though Evan knew she hadn't meant to, Chris's words surprised him, even hurt a little. Was he really that bad? Did he always see the down side? He scratched his head and gazed out the window. "No, I guess not."

"What happened?" Her voice was gentle, but it didn't stop him from feeling uncomfortable with the question. He never talked about the past; he'd found it to be a waste of time.

"My turn, huh?" he said wryly. "Any way you'll accept a large no-comment as an answer?"

"Hey, Evan, come on." Chris slanted him a mock-reproachful look. "I haven't stopped yakking about myself. I swear, you know more about me than anyone. I'm sick to death of me—now I want to know about you."

"What exactly is it you want to know?"

"Everything."

Looking down, he frowned as he traced a finger over the curlicues in the pink Formica tabletop. "We were farmers, and dirt poor. I have a younger brother, Lon. He's in the merchant marine."

"Are you two close?"

"When we were kids, yeah. We don't see each other that much anymore. Christmas sometimes."

"And your parents?"

"My dad died, and I'm not sure about my mother. She ran off when I was pretty young. Five or six."

"Oh, Evan, how awful for you."

The look of compassion on Chris's face was why he hated talking about himself. That hollow, lonely feeling came up—the one he'd had, it seemed, forever. But he had to tell Chris at least something about himself. After all her confessions, he knew he owed it to her, even if it brought up old ghosts, older regrets.

"Yeah, I missed my mother a lot," he said, studying a fingernail. "For a while anyway. She used to read to me; in fact, I guess she's the reason I became a writer. There were always books around, and she encouraged Lon and me to use our imaginations." He smiled, but there was no happiness in it. "Mostly, I imagined myself out of that town. I hated it."

"Why?"

"It was too dry there, too small. After my mother left, my dad's drinking got worse, and Lon and I ran wild. The three of us were the town's favorite topic of gossip."

He looked up to see her watching and listening intently. "Look, I guess it wasn't all bad. There were some good times, some nice memories. But still, I got away as soon as I could. I came out to L.A. before I was twenty. With my wife."

She raised an eyebrow. "You've been married?"

He shrugged. "It was a long time ago, or it feels like it anyway. It's history."

The waitress set down the ice cream sodas. Evan dipped a spoon into his and ate some foam without tasting it. "It's as if it were another life. You know that feeling? Looking back on yourself after you've grown up and changed?"

"As though it had happened to someone else," Chris said with a nod. "Oh, yes, I know the feeling well."

Evan smiled hopefully. "So, have I talked enough about myself yet?"

"Not even close." Chris took a sip of her soda, then wiped her upper lip with a napkin. "Your wife. Tell me about her."

Evan gazed out the window again. Two teenage girls wearing short skirts, tight sweaters, and absurdly high platform shoes walked by. "She was beautiful," he said, "with a fragile quality, like a . . . sad angel. She lived on the next farm over."

"You grew up together?"

"Yeah. She always tagged along after me, told me one day she would marry me. I used to tell her to get lost, but she stuck to me like glue. Couldn't get rid of her." He met Chris's clear gray gaze. "After a while I guess I stopped trying. Her name was Sue Ann. She changed it to Suzanna when we got here."

Chris studied Evan's face as he spoke. It was unsmiling, unsentimental, almost expressionless. What was she looking for? she asked herself. Some key to figuring him out? The reason he had such a protective wall around himself? Some hint of vulnerability?

She took another sip of her soda. "How did you wind up in L.A.?"

"Sue Ann and I ran away to Vegas and got married. We worked there awhile, then just continued on west till we got here. It was pretty rough. We were always short of money, but then, we were both used to that. I never did get to college, which I'd wanted to do my whole life, but"—his mouth formed a hint of a smile—"what the hell, I've done all right."

"So it seems."

"I held down two jobs and got into a writing program at one of the studios while Sue Ann tried to get work modeling. I didn't find out about the drugs until it was too late. But I tried."

"Oh, Evan."

He stared sightlessly out the window again, his jaw tensing, and Chris had a feeling she was being shown just a hint of his deep wells of raw regret.

"Do you know what this town does to young girls with great faces and bodies?" he said. "It eats them alive. It's become a cliché, but it's true. She held out for almost a year, trying to be the faithful, supportive wife. But she wasn't very strong, never had been."

"What happened?"

"Some casting guy shoved powder up her nose and told her she had a brilliant future. And she bought it, even though she really had no acting talent. I mean none. She got in front of a camera and she froze. Poor kid," he mused with a distant compassion, "except for her face, she really didn't have a lot going for her in the Hollywood sense."

"Except you."

His laugh was humorless. "Yeah, lucky her. I couldn't do a thing to help her, though I certainly tried. We divorced and she took off for Europe. She's still there, I guess. I last talked to her three or four years ago. She called me up from somewhere in Spain. Said she needed money for a rehab program. I told her I'd gladly pay it, but I would send the money to the clinic directly. She told me to get lost, then told me a bunch of other things I could do to myself. I finally hung up on her."

Chris felt the tears in the back of her throat. Tears for Sue Ann, of course, but mostly for the man who had tried with all his heart to be enough for her and who, in spite of his denial, was still punishing himself for having failed.

She shook her head. "Oh, Evan, what a waste."

"Yes." He took a sip of water and frowned. "Chris, I'm not good at this talking stuff."

"You're doing fine. One more question?"

He exhaled loudly. "All right. One."

"Do you still love her?" she asked softly, holding her breath just a little, afraid to hear the answer.

Sadness crossed his face for a fleeting moment, then it was gone. "No, that ended a long time ago."

She gave a silent sigh of relief. "But you still feel responsible for her."

"No, not that either." He met her gaze directly. "I don't feel much of anything. Not anymore."

"Don't you?"

"Chris," he said, his brows knitting as he reached for her hand. "Sometimes, with you, I—"

He didn't finish the thought. Instead, he looked down at the tabletop and cursed softly. "Oh, hell. I wish things were different. I wish I were different. But I'm not."

He brought her hand up to his mouth and kissed the palm lightly. "Okay. Enough soul-baring. Ready for a surprise?"

The rapid-fire change of subject threw her for a loop. She wanted to hear more about just what it was that Evan wished were different. But she'd probably pushed enough for one sitting.

"Surprise?" she said.

"Guess where we're going now?"

"The Universal Studios tour?"

He winced. "Spare me. That's for tourists, not for insiders like us."

——◆————◆——

Evan got them on the set of *Tulip & Co.*, a TV show that was not one of Chris's favorites but one she watched occasionally. It was about a group of twentysomethings who all worked at the same trendy apparel shop, and slept, fought, and broke up with one another regularly.

When she and Evan strolled onto the huge sound-stage, a couple of people waved and said hello to him. He introduced Chris to the cast and crew as a visitor from Colorado—making no mention of her fifteen minutes of fame, thank heaven—but kept his arm around her shoulder possessively.

Carla Carroll, the extremely well-endowed redheaded star of the show, smiled at Chris briefly, then smiled a little longer at Evan. He gave the actress no encouragement—which delighted Chris—but she couldn't help wondering.

"Evan," Chris whispered moments later as they stood under a large light pole, observing various people scurrying around to set up a shot.

"Yes?"

"I saw the way Carla looked at you, and I want to ask you how well you know her, but I don't know if I should."

"So, are you asking me? Do you really want to know?"

"No . . . Yes . . . I don't know."

"Come with me." He led her to a quiet corner of the soundstage, motioning her to sit in a canvas chair while he leaned against a wooden table facing her. "Here's the deal, Chris. I've lived in L.A. for a long time, and this business is pretty inbred. I've been to bed with my fair share—" He paused dramatically. "But not with Carla Carroll."

"Whew. Good."

She felt stupid for prying like that. She really had no claim on Evan. Worrying her bottom lip, she wondered again if she'd made a big mistake coming to L.A., winding up in Evan's bed, and telling him her secrets.

"Quiet on the set!" called out the assistant director.

Chris turned to see the actors in place for the next scene. A makeup person blotted Carla's nose, then scooted out of the shot. "Ready!" shouted the A.D. A bell clanged, the red Recording light lit up over all the doors, and a man with a clapboard and chalk announced the show, the scene, and the take.

"Action!"

Chris tried to keep her attention on the scene being filmed, but her thoughts kept drifting back to Evan.

In spite of all her best intentions, all her "why not live in the moment" pep talks to herself, she was in love with him. And he'd as much as told her that "love" hadn't been part of his vocabulary for a long, long while. A Do Not Touch sign had glowed across Evan's forehead from the beginning, in fact.

In replaying their earlier conversation at the coffee shop, Chris thought she now understood Evan's message loud and clear. He wished he were different, he'd said . . . but he wasn't.

What he was was every woman's worst nightmare. He was drop-dead good-looking, funny and interesting, and made love to her as though she were the most important thing in the universe. But—and it was a pretty bit "but" —she knew she couldn't have him. Not really, not in any permanent way. He was the type who ran for his life the first time a woman mentioned words like "commitment" and "relationship."

The unavailable man.

She snuck a peek at him. He was propped against the table, his arms draped over his chest, that shuttered look on his face. If she didn't know him, she would think him arrogant. But she did know him, knew much more about him now than he wanted her to. Evan protected himself by assuming an air of not giving a damn.

She wanted him to give a damn. About her.

Chris's attention was drawn back to the set when one of the actors flubbed his lines, let out a stream of profanities, then blushed. To the sound of good-natured laughter, the scene was stopped and restarted. Chris rested her elbows on her knees and kept watching.

Evan glanced at her. He wasn't exactly bored—with Chris anywhere in the vicinity, that was impossible. But he didn't want to be here. He'd never found the filming of a script as interesting as the creating of one, and the finished product was never anything like he'd imagined when he wrote it.

But Chris was taking it all in. She inspected the positioning and shading of the lights, the careful placement of both the overhead and body microphones. She mentioned how different the colors on the monitors seemed from the way they appeared on the set. Yeah, it was obvious she was hooked on show biz. The lure was pretty hard to resist, though he couldn't help wishing she were one of the ones who weren't even tempted.

In the middle of the seventh take of the same scene, Evan muttered under his breath, "They're not going to get any better, so why bother?"

Chris sidled up to him. "You don't want to be here, do you?" she whispered in his ear, her low, smooth voice pouring through his veins like honey. "And you're suffering through it for me. Now it's my turn. What can I do for you?"

He gave her a sly look. "You mean that?"

"Yes."

"Come with me."

ELEVEN

As soon as the A.D. yelled "Cut!" Evan pushed open the rear door of the soundstage and he and Chris left. They were in a long corridor with rooms on both sides. People hurried by, clipboards and costumes and notepads in hand. Evan grabbed Chris's hand and pulled her past the communal makeup room with its three barber chairs, pots, pencils, and brushes on a long table, and rows of lights above the mirror. They passed a lounge with several sofas and chairs, then a couple of offices and a room filled with cables and wires and lights, till they reached the end of the corridor where there were six dressing rooms, three on each side.

Evan pulled Chris into the first unoccupied room, and closed the door behind them.

The dressing room was small and obviously not in use; apart from the bare table, the only other furniture was a chair and an empty clothes rack.

"Evan?" Chris said.

He put a finger to his mouth, signaling that she needed to be quiet, and backed her against a wall. He grabbed both her wrists and raised them over her head. Then he lowered his mouth to hers and kissed her till her knees felt weak.

When she was able to come up for air, she whispered, "Wh-what are you doing?"

"Kissing you, with the intention of doing a lot more," he answered in a sleepy, sexy voice.

"Now? Here?"

"Now and here. In a dressing room in the middle of the day." He smiled. "You asked what you could do for me. This is it."

She giggled. "But there are people all around."

"That's what makes it exciting."

"What if someone tries to come in?"

He reached over and flipped the lock on the door handle. "They won't be able to."

"But the walls are thin, aren't they? What if someone hears us?"

"We'll have to do our best so they don't. Think of it as a challenge. We can work on our pantomime skills."

His eyes held a devilish gleam as he grabbed her by the waist and lifted her onto the dressing table. The sense of anticipation in the air was even more heightened as Chris leaned back against the mirror and watched Evan flick on the rows of lights at the top and sides of the vanity.

"Why did you do that?" she whispered.

"So I can see you," he said so softly that she found herself reading his lips.

"Oh."

"So I can watch your face and your body," he went on, removing her shoes, "while you try not to make any noise."

"You too," she whispered. "You have to be quiet too."

"I look forward to it."

He sat down in the chair facing her, and pushed her skirt up to the tops of her thighs. "Good. No hose."

"I'll never wear hose again."

"Smart move. But what have we here?" He ran a fingertip around the elastic of her panties.

"They're called bikinis." How magical his hands were. Already her skin was heated, prickling with antici-pation; already she was finding breathing more and more difficult. "I bought them in a semi-naughty store in Den-ver . . . oh! . . . before I got here. And some other stuff you haven't seen yet."

He chuckled softly. "A woman who thinks ahead. Did you buy them for me?"

"For me. I didn't know what would happen with you."

"But you thought about it? About being with me?" He stroked his fingertips across her stomach and around the tops of her thighs with a light, teasing touch. "Like this?"

"The truth?"

"The truth."

"Oh, Evan," she gasped as his thumbs worked their way under the elastic of her panties and caressed the soft, silky hair there. "It was all I thought about."

"Yeah, I know the feeling."

He bent his head and ran his tongue over one knee, then along the inside of her thigh. "I hope you don't mind if I dispense with too much foreplay," he whispered, then moved his attentions farther up her thigh.

"No." She moaned audibly, then put her hand over her mouth. "Oops, sorry. No, I don't think I mind at all."

Evan pulled the wisp of silk down her legs and tossed it aside, then moved his chair in closer and clasped her buttocks in his large hands. "You know that little growling sound you make right before you—"

"I do not growl," she interrupted.

"You do growl, trust me. Remember how thin the walls are. No matter how much you want to cry out, don't." Those were the last words she heard from him before his mouth, tongue, and teeth found the womanly folds between her legs and her small nub of sensuality.

It was amazing what an aphrodisiac the challenge of enforced silence was. Chris alternated between gripping the edge of the table with her hands and grabbing Evan's hair as she squirmed restlessly, biting down on her lower lip in an effort not to articulate her pleasure. All the energy that was being suppressed found its way to her skin and muscles and nerve endings in a heightened, almost unbearable rush of torrid sensations.

It was amazing, too, how quickly, how easily Evan brought her to a fever pitch, how her hips undulated on the table, grinding into his hands, thrusting upward to meet whatever pleasure he chose to give.

And it was amazing how, in the final moments, his finger reached high into the deep moist recesses of her as his thumb and tongue stroked her slowly and insistently, tantalizing her flesh until she couldn't stand the tension anymore.

She came apart. She put a hand over her mouth as she did, but a long cry sprang from deep inside her, and between that and the way the table was shaking and thumping from the movement of her body, Chris knew that no one passing by would have any doubt about what was happening behind the closed dressing room door.

She shuddered through a dazed, sensual afterglow while Evan kissed her hands and thighs and murmured how special she was, how magical her responses to him were.

She opened her eyes to find him gazing up at her, his arms folded across her thighs.

"Did I growl?" she said.

"I have no idea."

Tenderly, she brushed a few strands of hair off his forehead. "Oh, Evan," she said, "that was . . . astonishing."

He ran his tongue slowly around his mouth. "I love the taste of you," he whispered.

She blushed and shuddered some more. No one in her life had ever been as openly sensual with her as this man was, or had ever brought out this unashamed, blatantly lusty side of her.

He captured her hand and brought it to his mouth for a kiss. "I guess we'd better vacate the premises."

He found her panties and helped her off the table. While she adjusted her clothing, Evan headed for the door and was about to turn the knob when Chris said, "Hold it right there, cowboy."

He turned and looked at her questioningly. "What?"

She walked over to him, took his hands in hers, and led him back to the chair. "Sit."

He did. "Why?"

"No questions, please. Just do as you're told."

"But—"

"Shh."

She knelt in front of him and slanted a teasing look up at him. "If I remember correctly, I asked what I could do for you. And you—foolish man, not to take advantage of a great offer like that—proceeded to give me a ride to paradise."

"That *was* for me."

"I believe you. And this is for me."

She unsnapped his jeans and slowly lowered the zipper.

"Chris?" Evan said.

She looked up at him, her movement stilled by the tone of his voice. "Yes?"

The expression on his face was serious, intense. "I . . . can't make any promises."

"I haven't asked for any."

"Yeah, I know. But if you have any fears or worries about other women, put them away. It's never been like this with anyone else. Never."

Emotion tugged at the back of her throat and she nodded. "Me too."

He cupped her cheek in his hand and they stared at each other wordlessly for a few moments. Oh, Chris thought silently. Oh. Evan had just told her—in his way

—that he loved her. She tried to stop her heart from soaring, but it didn't want to listen.

Maybe. Just maybe . . .

Even with her head yelling at her not to make assumptions, she couldn't help wishing. Life was a series of possibilities, wasn't it? And in spite of how tough things had always been for her, she was still more the glass-is-half-full type.

Who knew what the future might bring? What she did know was that she had three more days away from reality. Three more days of loving and scripts and movieland and ocean views. And Evan.

The tender way he was looking at her brought tears to her eyes. This was why she'd been able to trust him almost from the beginning, because of this strong connection between them. Love.

Chris swallowed the lump in her throat and gave him a smile from deep inside. Then she turned her attention once again to his zipper. She took her time lowering it, savoring the way his erection grew as she did. She took him in her hand and stroked up and down, from base to tip, with her thumbs.

His intake of breath made her smile with womanly satisfaction. He was full and thick and ready, and she gazed up at him through lowered lids.

"My turn," she whispered. "And, Evan, remember not to make any noise."

Tapping a pencil on his desk, Evan looked up from the yellow pad in front of him and glanced over at Chris. She was ensconced in his tacky old armchair, the one he kept in his home office for sentimental reasons and refused to have recovered or reupholstered. Buster was resting his snout on her knees, wagging his tail as he gazed up at her with total and abject adoration. Chris's face was morning-fresh and peaceful. Her hair was still damp, and the sun that streamed in the windows lit on a few individual just-dry strands, making them glisten.

Evan wanted the world to stop right there and then, because he knew the moment was perfect, and perfect moments never lasted.

"Chris?"

"Hmm?" She continued to scratch behind the dog's ears, smiling with amusement at the look of bliss on the animal's face.

"I need to get some more details about the night of the robbery. Do you mind?"

She looked up at him with surprise.

They'd worked most of Friday, then had dinner at Morton's. Chris's head could have been on a swivel with all the ogling she'd done at the famous and notorious who dined there. Afterward he'd brought her back to his place to spend the night because she'd said she missed seeing the waves. They'd woken up an hour earlier and he'd put on the coffee while Chris made her daily call to her kids.

They'd been sipping coffee in his office—she fresh from a shower and dressed in his robe, he in an old pair of sweats—talking about the difference between dogs and cats, the shameless dependence of one and the frustrating independence of the other. Evan's question had been an abrupt change of subject.

"Uh, okay," she said. "I guess we'll work on the script now."

"Sorry," he said. "That's the way it happens sometimes. For most writers. We talk about one thing while the brain is processing something entirely different. When the processing is over, it pops out."

"Kind of like a toaster oven, I guess. So, all this morning you've been mulling over the script?"

"I guess I have."

"*All* this morning?"

He grinned at her, knowing she was referring to the sensual wake-up call she'd given him. He held up his hands in a don't-blame-me fashion. "Hey, I'm not responsible for my subconscious."

"A likely story."

"I'm afraid when I'm on a project—" He shrugged. "My mind is working pretty much full-time, whether I want it to or not. But the good news is, I think I have a pretty fine outline now."

"There?" She pointed to the yellow pad on his desk.

He tapped the side of his head. "Here. I'll make a few more notes and then write it up more formally. Okay?"

She got that look on her face, the one that said she still wasn't sure if her secrets were safe, although she did seem to relax about it a little more each day. Curling her legs up under her, she covered her bare feet with his robe. Buster gave a sigh at being displaced and plopped down on the rug nearby. Chris smiled at the dog, then lifted a cup from the small table next to her chair, took a sip, and said, "Fire away."

Evan swiveled his chair around to face her, hunching

over and resting his elbows on his knees. "Now, let's get this straight. If it's too painful, you don't have to talk about what happened that night. Not a word if you don't want to. I know some of the story, and what I don't know we can fill in from police reports, eyewitness accounts, and a little dramatic license. In fact, if you'd rather, we'll consider the subject of that night closed permanently."

"Thanks for saying that, but I don't mind, really," she said. "Not since I told you all about it back in Loman. It was like a catharsis."

"Good, because it's a major centerpiece, a pretty dramatic one. It'll be the final thirty, thirty-five minutes of the script."

"Out of how many minutes? One hundred twenty?"

He chuckled. "Hardly. In a two-hour teleplay, there are actually ninety-six minutes of script. You have to leave about twenty-four minutes for commercials, station breaks, opening and closing credits, promos for upcoming shows, stuff like that."

"I see. So, that night at the convenience store will be about—what?—a third of the script. What's going to be in the other two-thirds?" There was a hint of trepidation in her voice, and more than ever he wanted to ease her fears.

He sat up and took a sip of coffee from the large mug on his desk, then set it down again. Propping his elbows on the sides of his chair, he steepled his fingers and studied Chris. "I'm thinking that the main theme, the main idea the whole story will revolve around, will be something you told me. Remember the first thing that flashed through your mind when the kid put the gun to your head?"

She nodded. "How can I forget? 'My God, my children will be orphans.'"

"Yeah," he said quietly, moved even now by the way Chris said the words, and knowing that he could imagine only a small part of what she must have been feeling at the time. "The orphan theme. How you would do anything so your children would never have to experience the same feelings you did—the isolation, the loneliness, the need to belong. That's going to be the hook.

"And don't worry," he said as he saw her frown of concern, "it won't be anything embarrassing, I promise."

"Better not be," she warned, only half kidding, he could tell.

"Trust me. I'm not into emotional, self-indulgent writing. I figure if you do a hearts-and-flowers kind of thing, there's nothing left for the audience to do—you rob them of their own honest reactions." He smiled self-consciously. "End of diatribe. Thank you, Mr. Stone, you may now descend from your soapbox."

"Boy," Chris said, shaking her head, "Marla did one good thing, didn't she?"

"What's that?"

"Hired you instead of someone who might make me cringe with shame."

He leaned over and took one of her hands in his. "She did another good thing too," he said softly. "She brought us together."

"That she did."

They gazed at each other for a couple of moments,

then Chris seemed to get uncomfortable. She removed her hand from his and took a sip of coffee. "Hey, aren't we supposed to be working?"

He frowned. "Chris? Anything wrong?"

"Nope. It's just that time's a-wasting. I leave tomorrow, remember?"

He wished she hadn't said that; he'd been trying to forget. She would be leaving, and he hated the thought. Evan had never felt more alive, more attuned to the world around him. And less negative, it seemed. Moved easily. Emotions rushed through him like a waterfall. This was new territory for him, and didn't always sit well in his insides.

What if this time with Chris were only a magical break from reality and as soon as she was gone, he would find himself back in his former isolated state? He didn't like that thought any more than he liked the thought of her leaving. Well then, what was he going to do about it?

Evan scowled as he glanced at the notes on his desk. He hated all this ambivalence.

"Evan? Are you okay?"

Maybe it was better to get back to work. He looked up from his notes and gave her what he hoped was a reassuring smile. "Sure. How about if I tell you what I have so far?"

"All right."

"We open with a close-up of a woman—Marla—a gun at her head, terror in her eyes. A voice-over—Marla again, as you—says 'My God, my children will be orphans.' Then there's a ripple effect, a wavy screen that indicates a flashback or memory, and we're on a shot of a baby in a basket. A foundling—you. The credits will roll over this. We follow some of your childhood, the foster homes, the loneliness. Nothing about time in lock-up or any real trouble with the law, just harmless kid stuff."

Evan looked up from his notes and met Chris's gaze. "Okay so far?"

She seemed to be waiting. "So far."

"Is this upsetting you?"

"Not yet."

"Please, trust me."

"I wouldn't be here if I didn't."

He nodded. "Good. Here's how we fudge over the cult and pregnancy thing. I'm envisioning a scene with the kid at the Greyhound station, but he has nothing to do with a cult. He's just a good-looking, screwed-up teenager. We play it like you two are both sixteen and are attracted to each other. Maybe you get a Coke and talk, or a stroll along the river. We use a bunch of close-ups and reactions, so we know you two are going to get together. We never even mention Arizona, by the way; this all takes place in Chicago."

"Keep going, I'm liking this more and more."

"I'm glad." That subtle tension that had been in the room was just about gone now, and Evan breathed a silent sigh of relief. "After the coffee-shop scene we cut to you hitching a ride to Denver, chatting with Tory. You fill in the missing couple of years with dialogue. You tell her that you married too young, made a mistake, got out in time, and are thinking of starting over in a new city."

"Which is what happened."

"Right. You're planning on putting the baby up for

adoption as you start your new life. You look out the car window into the night, scared but excited at the same time. End of act one."

"End of act one?"

"Scripts," he explained, "most of them anyway, have a kind of three-act structure, each act propelling the story forward and continuing the theme. Your story lends itself well to the main theme: a young mother determined that no matter what, her child—then children," he amended, "when you have Lisa—will never go through what she did."

"Yeah," Chris said thoughtfully. "And again, that's kind of the way it was."

"The closer we stick to the truth, the better it will be dramatically." He consulted his notes again. "Act two: The cute meeting with John—you're overtired, over-worked, young baby at home, your studies, two jobs. So you spill eggs on him. It's a nice scene."

"Glad you like it," she said dryly.

He smiled at her humor and took a sip of his coffee. "And then the meeting with your in-laws. We'll have to fudge some more there, make Dora a warmer mother figure."

Chris laughed. "Really, Evan, she's not so bad. Just kind of abrupt."

"Yeah, right. Whatever you say. Then we follow the time line pretty much as it happened. The birth of Lisa. A scene with you teaching school. The tragic death of John. Maybe a scene at the hospital when you realize that you're it, the only parent they have left, and you can't take any chances with your life. If you wanted to try skydiving or free-falling, it's no longer a good idea. Not till the kids are grown anyway. They must not be or-phaned."

Chris stared at him with a look of wonder on her face. "It's uncanny. What you just said, that's exactly what went through my mind after John died. Even the skydiv-ing part. How did you know?"

He shrugged. "I guess I just closed my eyes and put myself in your place." He consulted the pad. "So, John's death is the end of act two. Act one is three to five scenes, plus a montage of foster homes; about thirty minutes. Act two is five to eight scenes, thirty-four or -five minutes.

"Which brings us to act three—the night of the rob-bery—which will be done in two sections, I think. The events that got you to the store, and the robber's appear-ance, then the moment when you realize you have to take action and the action you take. This part will build well, I think, with a lot of fast cuts and suspense. And when you and I have talked about it a bit more, I'll have a better idea of the details."

Looking off into space, Chris played with the belt of Evan's robe. She seemed to be considering everything he'd said, and he found himself holding his breath, won-dering if talking about his craft like this, stripping away the mystery, had somehow changed the way she saw him.

Wait a minute. Was he honestly thinking that Chris wanted to be with him only because he was a professional scriptwriter? He dismissed the thought as not worthy of either of them. But still, he was feeling insecure, vulnera-ble in a way that was totally foreign to him. Why? he wondered silently. His need for approval from her? The short time they had left together?

After a while Chris favored him with a soft smile. "I'm no expert, but I think the story you've come up with is quite wonderful. And I feel honored that you've let me in on how you do what you do. And most amazing of all, you've managed to keep all my secrets."

"I promised I would."

"You sure did." Nodding slowly, Chris rose from her chair and walked over to him, a look of gratitude, and something more, on her face. "My hero."

Placing his hands on her waist, Evan gazed up at her. "So," he couldn't help saying, "you're pleased."

"Most definitely. Yes."

He pulled her in between his legs and hugged her tightly. His heart felt absurdly light as he basked in her approbation. Funny, he hadn't looked to a woman for a compliment—about his work or anything else—since he'd been a small child. "Good."

She stroked his hair. "Tired of me yet?"

"Not even close. You?"

"I'll let you know," she said, and he could hear the smile in her voice. Then she leaned back and regarded him, her expression serious. "So now, what about Marla?"

"What about her?"

"Am I out of danger there? Will the story satisfy her?"

"Are you kidding? She's in every scene. That's all that's important."

Chris laughed with delighted relief. "Well, good, then."

"In fact, I gave her two juicy crying scenes. She'll think she's died and gone to heaven."

"She likes to cry?"

"On camera, for sure. Marla's a great crier—she can do it on cue. That's how she got the job on *The Family Finch*."

"Really? Ooh, an inside Hollywood story." She leaned over and kissed his cheek, then plopped herself down on his lap. "Tell me."

He put his arms around her waist. "Well, at the audition for the show—she was five? six?—they asked her if she could pretend to weep hysterically for the camera, and offered her that artificial stuff that a lot of actors use. But it wasn't necessary. She promptly burst into tears and kept it up. She just wouldn't stop, not even when they told her that they'd seen enough. Not until they whipped out a contract for her father to sign. Then those tears dried up on the spot."

Chris laughed with delight. "Is that story true?"

"It's possible that it's what they call an apocryphal show-biz tale." Evan lifted an eyebrow and shrugged. "But I wouldn't put it past her. Marla's always been pretty ambitious. Her killer instinct is awesome, which you are in a position to know firsthand."

"That I am. Well, gosh, I've learned a lot."

"Have you?"

"Sure. Actresses love to cry. A two-hour movie isn't two hours. The truth can be disguised and still be the truth. And there are themes and act breaks in movies . . . in life too."

Her mood was playful, but that strain he'd noticed earlier was still hovering in the background. He thought he'd taken care of her worries about the script. "Chris? Are you sure everything's okay?"

"Absolutely. How about feeding me while we work?" she said brightly. "Or I'll feed you. I'm a good cook, by the way. Best pancake maker this side of the Mississippi. We can fix breakfast and I'll tell you everything I can remember about the robbery. Act three, as you call it."

With a quick grin Chris jumped up from his lap. Evan wondered if he was imagining that almost manic undertone he was sensing in her. "Where are you getting all this energy from?"

"Must have something to do with the California sunshine." Raising her arms over her head, she stretched quickly, then went over to the window and peered out. "Another beautiful day in paradise. Oh, by the way"—she turned and faced him—"I have a request."

"Sure."

"After the party, can we spend tonight, our last night together, at the hotel? I really love those little chocolates they put on the pillow. And I want to make a phone call from the bathtub. And I have a few more semi-naughty pieces of lingerie I'd like to model for you."

"Request granted, most emphatically."

"In fact"—was it his imagination, or was her voice shaking?—"I should get over there a couple of hours before the party so I can make myself gorgeous."

He got up from his chair and walked over to her,

encircling her waist with his arms. "You don't have to make any effort to be gorgeous. You already are."

She rested her hands on his shoulders and turned her soft gray-eyed gaze on him. "Keep them compliments coming. I love them. And I love you."

TWELVE

The silence that hung in the air after Chris said the words felt endless. She kept her eyes on Evan's face, checking for his reaction to the Pandora's box she'd opened. It wasn't good.

"Chris," he said finally. "I don't know—"

"No, don't," she interrupted, all her previous high spirits gone just like that. "I didn't mean it to come out that way. I'm not sorry it did, mind you, but— Well, I guess maybe I am sorry."

"Why?"

"Because of the look on your face right now. The one that says you don't know if you should take me in your arms or head for the hills."

"That transparent again, huh?"

"Yes." She turned her back to him and gazed out the window. The day didn't seem nearly as sunny as it had just moments before.

"Chris, I want to be honest with you. I feel . . .

more for you than I've ever felt for anyone, but there's something holding me back from, well, taking it any further. . . ."

Chris closed her eyes. Her shoulders slumped with disappointment. She'd allowed herself to hope, and look where it had gotten her.

Oh, how she wanted Evan to come up behind her and slip his arms around her waist and soothe her with words about how whatever it was, they'd work it out, about how he was willing to make a leap of faith because what he felt for her warranted it. But she was pretty sure that wouldn't happen, and his continued lack of response told her she was right on the money.

"Anyhow," she said after a long while, still looking out Evan's office window, "I guess that's that."

"I want to feel what you feel." She could hear the frustration in his voice. "Maybe I do . . . except I'm not sure if I even believe it's possible."

"And, silly me, I've gotten through life by believing in things that don't seem possible."

She wished she were one of those women who took things like this in stride, wished she could pretend that what had happened wasn't really that big a deal. But she never lied to herself. And what she was experiencing was deep, gut-wrenching pain, and, Lord, it hurt like crazy.

"Look," she said, hoping that the lump in her throat wouldn't prevent her from speaking. "I've changed my mind. I'd like to go back to the hotel now."

"Chris—"

She whirled around to face him and held up a hand. "Don't, Evan. It's okay, we've both been honest with each other, and there's no need to say anything else. I'm going to take you up on your offer to make up the details about the night of the robbery, and I'm going to treat myself to a nap and a long bath and a little time alone. Okay?"

She saw the concern on his face give way to that shuttered, defensive look. "If you say so."

"I mean," she went on with as much bravado as she could muster, "it's not often a schoolteacher from Colorado gets a Hollywood party in her honor. I don't intend to let anything interfere with me having the time of my life."

Marla's house was in the hills above Beverly Hills, at the end of a long, winding private driveway. A red-coated valet opened the limo door for Chris and helped her step out onto the pavement. Inside, it was just as Chris had imagined it would be—like something featured on *Lifestyles of the Rich and Famous*. She took in a foyer with marble floors, crystal chandeliers, two winding staircases, and expensive Oriental rugs.

A sudden attack of nerves made her duck into a nearby powder room and lock the door behind her. She checked her glossy red lipstick in the mirror, then she stepped back to get the full view. Except for the sadness around the eyes and the way her mouth kept drooping, she thought she looked her best. The decision to buy a new dress this afternoon had been the right one.

When she'd returned to the hotel, she'd been overwhelmed by depression, especially when she glanced at the dress she'd brought with her from Colorado. It was boring. All of her clothing was boring, she decided. Sensible. Modest. Easy to care for. Boring.

She'd never been one of those women who went shopping to cure the blues, but thought maybe it was time to give it a try. Taking a cue from *Pretty Woman*, Chris had asked the hotel manager where she could buy a really terrific, bona fide evening gown. He'd recommended a couple of places, arranged for a taxi, and sent her on her way. The salespeople had been so nice and helpful not only with the dress, but with all the accessories too.

In the mirror now she could see the result of her expedition, and it was worth every penny of the ridiculous amount of money she'd spent. Her dress was covered with gray and silver beads that reflected light and made the fabric shimmer. It was cut fairly low in front and very low in back, held up by thin silk straps. The skirt came to mid-thigh and was slightly flared, so it swung fluidly from side to side as she moved. Her hair was piled on top of her head in casual curls with several loose strands falling gracefully onto her neck. Long jet and silver earrings, black hose, and black three-inch heels completed the outfit.

Briefly she wondered what Evan's opinion would be, then assured herself it didn't really matter. She'd told him he needn't bother picking her up for the party, that Marla was sending a limo. Would he even show? she wondered. He hated parties, he'd told her, which didn't exactly surprise her. The man was a loner and a cynic and a lot of other things; she was better off without him.

She stood back and studied herself one final time, then shook her head with wonder. Whatever would the folks back home think if they could see her now? In the glass there was absolutely no trace of the small-town schoolteacher she'd been just a few days before. She had gone through some sort of metamorphosis, and she suspected the change went deeper than the clothes she wore.

Evan was responsible for some of that change, and she was candid enough to admit it. If she saw him, she would thank him.

Lord, how she wanted to see him again.

No, no, that wasn't what she was really feeling. What she wanted was for him to stay away from the party, to stay away from her.

She hoped she would never see him again in her life.

Get a grip, Chris said to the woman in the mirror. These mood swings she'd been experiencing all day— from exhilaration to sadness, from humiliation to defiance to downright hostility—they were just part of the letdown. The end of the vacation, the end of the dream.

That morning she'd experienced the classic nightmare, the one where one says "I love you" and the other doesn't.

She would put it out of her mind right this minute. Tonight she was going to a party. Tomorrow she was going back to her real life. She would square her shoulders and make the best of it. After all, she'd had lots of practice at that. She'd been making the best of it all her life.

She exited the powder room and made her way to what would be called the backyard. The word seemed inadequate here. Marla's pool was three times the size of Evan's, and had small candles in flower-shaped holders floating on the surface. There were tiny white lights in the trees, a tennis court off to one side, a series of dressing rooms on the other, and beyond that a huge patio with a one-hundred-eighty-degree view of L.A.

A banquet table was covered with food. White-coated waiters with trays of hors d'oeuvres circulated among the guests; Chris figured there were at least a hundred people out there. A full bar had been set up at the deep end of the pool, and as Chris's eyes scanned the faces in front of her, she tried to swallow down an acute case of nerves.

Oh, Lord, she thought, wasn't that Hal Carson over there? Talking with Melissa Wayne? And, oh, my heavens, Charlie Sawyer. Charlie Sawyer!

A familiar voice rang out. "Chris! You're here!"

Chris whipped around to see Marla barreling toward her. She wore tight satin pants, a sequined halter top, and platform shoes that had to be five inches high. She held both hands out in front of her as she came up to Chris and gave her a large hug, as though they were long-lost friends. Then Marla broke away and eyed her from the top of her curls to the bottom of her toes.

"Well, well, what a wonderful outfit!" Marla gushed. "Really, Chris, who ever would have thought you'd look like this? Four days in L.A. and what a change!"

Chris mentally recanted any previously charitable thoughts about Marla. The actress was making it sound as if during their earlier meetings Chris had resembled some lower life form.

She opened her mouth to say something cutting, but

the other woman was too quick for her. Marla clapped her hands loudly and turned to face her assembled guests. "Everyone! Please meet Chris McConnell, the *very* brave lady whose life I will be portraying next season."

There was some murmuring and scattered applause. A flashbulb went off, blinding Chris for a moment.

Marla went on. "There's a press kit on the table over by the bar, and a copy of some other material about Chris's story and the project. Please make sure you meet her during the evening. Right now we're going to get her a drink and some food, and then we'll be making the rounds. And thank you, all of you, for coming tonight. It means a lot."

Having finished her speech to the multitudes, Marla turned back to Chris and smiled warmly. "I mean it, Chris, you look terrific. But you seem so nervous. Has Evan been working you too hard? Come."

She took Chris by the hand and led her away.

Evan watched as Chris moved through the crush of celebrities with astonishing ease. With each new glass of champagne, with each eager, enthusiastic greeting and few moments of chat, his heart sank a little further. There was something about the way Chris was practically inhaling the exalted atmosphere of Marla's party that reminded him of Sue Ann. Too damned star-struck for her own good.

But Chris wasn't Sue Ann, and he knew it.

No, she was a lot stronger than Sue Ann, her ego a hell of a lot healthier.

And she looked great! Too great. She'd never worn anything this revealing—at least, not with him. He'd seen his share of shiny, clinging backless dresses—if you lived in L.A. long enough you saw it all—but not on someone like Chris. He wanted to smash the faces of the pompous, well-fed men who were eyeing her as though she were dessert. She was his, dammit.

But no, he amended, she wasn't his. He'd forfeited that right. That morning she'd laid it on the line, been up front about her feelings, and he'd waffled, like a coward. He'd blown it.

He was angry, at himself and at the situation. He probably shouldn't have come, shouldn't have risked his temper exploding in some inappropriate manner. Damn, he thought, throwing back a brandy and waiting for it to relieve some of the chill that had nothing to do with the weather. He shouldn't have come.

Two hours after her arrival Chris had been introduced to actors, writers, producers, directors. Also a couple of athletes and pop singers, some with their own entourages. Marla made sure Chris's champagne glass was filled, then arranged for the two of them to be photographed with various luminaries—a famous gossip columnist, an entertainment reporter for CNN, a United States senator who was sponsoring a crime bill. The two women flanked a seven-foot basketball player, sat on the lap of a children's TV show host, and kissed the cheek of a comic with a rubbery face and wandering hands.

Chris kept glancing around, looking for Evan, but she

didn't see him anywhere. Then she would be whisked away to meet another Oscar winner, more aging beauties and sex goddesses, one more young actor who could have been a Gap model. She really knew her film lore, and here, sharing the same soil with her, were the artists she'd admired for years. If it hadn't been for all this emotional chaos about Evan, she would have been in film-buff heaven.

She spotted him finally, over in a corner, nursing a drink. He nodded to her and she nodded back, then laughed uproariously at whatever it was that was being said to her. She had no idea what it was, of course, but she wanted him to think she was having a fabulous time. All evening she'd been sipping her champagne, pretending she was as witty and glamorous as everyone around her. Funnily enough, people kept treating her as though she were. For tonight, at least, she was a star.

In fact, at that moment a well-known lawyer, an extremely overweight man with body odor, was breathing his onion breath on her and asking for details of her deal with Marla, as he had at various intervals during the evening. Once again Chris declined to answer, and once again he told her however much it was, he could have tripled it.

"Thank you, Mr. Shankman," she said, more and more feeling the dizzying effects of the champagne.

"Call me Al."

"Al. Thank you, but I don't need—"

"Evening, Chris. Al."

It was Evan, right behind her. Her smile froze in place.

"Hi, Evan," the lawyer said, looking past Chris. "You involved in this deal with Marla?"

"I'm writing the script."

"I've just been telling Chris here—"

"Sorry, Al, I need to borrow Chris myself for a bit."

Al Shankman shrugged and made his way to the buffet table. Chris remained where she was, not overly eager to face Evan.

"Having a nice time?" he asked.

She stiffened, then turned toward him. "A better one than you've been having," she said, "brooding over there in the corner."

"I don't brood. I observe."

"My apologies."

She stood back and looked him up and down. He wore a soft wool jacket of tiny brown and white checks, dark brown slacks, and a cream-colored silk shirt, open at the neck. It was sort of a lord-of-an-English-manor ensemble and, with Evan's distinctly American cowboy look, shouldn't have worked as well as it did. But then, the man could wear a moth-eaten ape costume and still make her toes curl with longing.

"Nice outfit," she said. "I've never seen you all cleaned up and in your party gear."

"I do this about once a century. And speaking of party gear, you look . . . enticing. It's a great dress, what there is of it."

His expression didn't match the compliment. In spite of all the attention Chris had been paid that evening, she experienced a moment of panic. She splayed her hand over her chest. "Too revealing?"

Evan wanted to kick himself for bringing that look of uncertainty to Chris's face. "Hey, ignore me. You look terrific," he admitted. "This is plain old jealousy talking. I don't want anyone else to see what I've seen."

Her moment of self-doubt seemed to vanish in an instant. She arched an eyebrow. "How un-nineties of you. Downright Victorian."

"Seems that way."

"So, now we know." Her eyes seemed to be slightly glazed. How much had she had to drink? he wondered. "Underneath Evan Stone's I-don't-give-a-damn exterior lies a seething cauldron of emotions."

She was slurring her words slightly too.

"That's kind of a purple way of putting it," he said, "but yeah. If you don't mind my asking, how much champagne have you had?"

She put her hand over her mouth and giggled. "Way too much. It's a good thing I'm not driving."

"I think you need a little fresh air," he said, taking her arm and steering her away from the party.

"But we're already outside."

"Yeah, but there are too many people. Come."

He led her to the edge of the patio beyond the dressing rooms. They stood with elbows resting on top of the railing that ran along the perimeter. They were alone here; the night stretched beyond them, a slight fog making the sky look smoky black. The twinkling lights of the valley were so fuzzy, Evan thought, it was as though he were looking through a smudged camera lens.

Soft rock music from the party drifted out over the

canyon. He wished he could enjoy himself, wished he didn't feel so wired, so on edge.

"You're really getting into this," he said, "aren't you? This whole party thing."

"And you never did? The truth now." Chris leaned toward him and poked a finger into his chest. "Years ago, the first time you were at a party like this, tell me you weren't just a little starry-eyed?"

"Probably," he admitted.

"And you had crushes, I know you did." She poked him again, a kind of physical punctuation to the point she was making. "A fantasy about one night with some blond movie star."

He grabbed her fingers to make her stop. "Sure, I had fantasies, like any kid has."

"Well, that's what this is." She pulled her hand away and gestured at the gathering behind them. "It's a fantasy, that's all. I know it's not real. But I'm awfully glad I came."

"Just as long as you don't go Hollywood on me."

"I don't think there's any danger of that."

He shrugged. "Who knows. The way things work in this town, you can start out as a poster child for the well-adjusted, then you get a whiff of the money and fame and power, and your values—hell, your whole personality—could be warped within months."

She peered out at the night and shook her head. "I hate it when you do this."

"Do what?"

"Get so cynical. If you feel that strongly about living in L.A., why do you stay?"

He felt his jaw tense, but he didn't reply.

"I mean," she went on, "I'm just trying to understand why someone would constantly subject himself to a place he hated."

"This is where I earn my living, so it's where I live. I love my work, believe it or not, so I put up with all of the things I hate about Hollywood. I live in Malibu, as far away from this whole scene as possible."

She turned to go, feeling too fragile for this confrontation, but he grabbed her upper arms and made her face him again.

"Now you tell me something," he continued, piercing her with his intense gaze. "Why do you live in that little town? You're not happy there, it's obvious."

Quick words of justification sprang to her lips. "It's where my work is." She paused. "And my children . . ."

"That's right."

Chris frowned, then nodded. "But you're right, I would like to live elsewhere, away from Loman. And I'm afraid to do anything about it."

"We're two of a kind, aren't we?" he said with a sad smile.

He let go of her arms, and she sagged against the railing. "I think I'd better sit down."

"Just a minute." Evan took off his jacket and spread it over the stone bench just behind them. "Okay."

Chris sank gratefully onto the seat. "Thanks."

He sat down next to her on the bench. Taking her hand in his, he said, "I didn't want to do this, I didn't want to ruin your party."

"You haven't ruined it."

His thumb stroked the soft skin across her knuckles. "I guess you hit a nerve. Because, of course, I've often asked myself why I do stay here."

"As you said, this is where your work is."

"That . . . but sometimes I think I deserve to be here with all these crazies."

Chris looked into Evan's eyes, saw the bleakness there, and all the anger she'd felt toward him, all the hurt, evaporated. She wished that she could make him a happier person, but she knew that no one could do that for anyone else.

"You don't deserve that," she said softly.

"No?"

"No."

He put his arm around her and she rested against his shoulder.

They didn't talk for a while. Chris's head was still swimming a little and she felt like going to sleep on the soft silk of Evan's shirt. But no, there was something important she wanted to say, an insight that had been forming since she'd come to L.A.

"Evan?"

"Hmm?"

"The people out here, in show business, I know their personalities are a little exaggerated—"

"A little?"

"Okay, a lot. But I don't think they're any more warped—warped," she repeated, licking her lips. "That's a hard word to say when your tongue doesn't work. What I mean is, you can become warped in Loman as easily as in Hollywood. It's not the place, it's the person."

"Whatever you say."

Lifting her head, she punched his rib lightly. "Don't be condescending."

"Sorry."

"But, Evan, think about it." She rested once again on his broad shoulder and felt him tighten his hold on her. "I mean, the secrets are more glamorous out here, that's all. The face-lifts and hair transplants. The whiff of marijuana from that dressing room behind us, and the way people go into dark corners and come out again a little later, adjusting their clothing."

"Observant, aren't you."

"It's hard to miss. But we've got secrets back home too. Our mayor—Frank?—wears lifts in his shoes. And you know why he never married? His mother. Before her death, he never went anywhere without her."

"That so?"

"One of the tellers in the bank—who shall remain nameless—has been carrying on with the bank president for years. They meet every week at the Bide-A-While Motel on Highway 12. Even the principal of my school takes a nip from a little bottle he keeps in his desk every time the bell rings, so that by the end of the day he's real peaceful.

"People are people. Out here they wear sequins, back home polyester. But they're the same all over. Good and bad, crazy and normal." She hiccuped and put her hand over her mouth. "Anyway, that's what I wanted to tell you. That's my opinion."

He kissed the top of her head. "Opinion noted."

"I'm talking too much, huh. It's the champagne."

Music from the party drifted passed them and disappeared into the night. An owl hooted; it sounded melancholy. Somewhere far off a dog barked. Neither Chris nor Evan spoke for a while.

Then he broke the silence. "I do love you, you know."

THIRTEEN

The words registered in her brain but didn't produce the expected soaring emotional reaction in her heart. "But you're not real happy about it," she said.

"Is that how I sound?"

"Downright funereal. Oh, Evan. Whatever are we going to do with you?"

"Probably ought to shoot me and put me out of my misery. I don't ever remember feeling so out of sorts, like my life is upside down."

"Why?" She was sobering up pretty rapidly now.

He squeezed her shoulder one more time, rose, and walked over to the edge of the patio. After looking out at the view for a few moments, he turned and leaned an elbow on the railing. "I thought I was all right. I thought I knew who I was and what I wanted. And then I met you, and suddenly I didn't know as much as I thought I did. I used to have a hard edge that I was sure I needed to stay alive. I knew that relationships didn't last very long, that love was something you couldn't count on."

Shaking his head, he looked down at his feet.

"And now?" Chris prompted.

"Now I can feel myself changing. And I'm not sure it's a good thing. I've lost that edge, I feel . . . softer somehow, not as tough as I used to be." He looked up and gazed at her, his hands fisted at his sides. "You've done it to me."

"And you don't know whether to throw your arms around me in gratitude or wring my neck."

"Something like that," he answered, unsmiling.

He sat down next to her again and gripped her hands. "Chris," he said, his voice filled with emotion, "I'm judgmental, arrogant, and jealous. I'm possessive. I'm jaded. I'm cynical. Why in hell would you want to love me?"

"Masochism?"

"This isn't funny."

"No, but you're being way too hard on yourself. Yes, you're probably everything you say you are, but you're also funny and talented and loving and sexy and you make me feel beautiful. I mean, those count for something, don't they?"

He shrugged. "But I haven't even mentioned the biggest drawback to loving me. I don't know if I can trust a woman."

She was stone cold sober by now, and she nodded. "True, but it's not hard to understand why. I mean, I'm no shrink, but it doesn't take a genius to figure out that your mother ran off, your wife ran off, most of the women you come in contact with want something from you—and they're probably a lot more like Marla than like Harriet Nelson—so you don't have a lot of expectations from my sex. Really, who can blame you? I—"

"Chris? Evan? Where are you two? Chris?" Marla's voice came from somewhere in back of them and broke the moment.

Evan muttered, "The woman has the worst timing."

"What do you think?" Chris whispered, putting her hand over her mouth. "Shall we hide? Or shall we let the wicked witch find us?"

"It's your party. You call it."

"Chris?" Marla was getting closer now. "Sean Peters is here, and he wants to say hello."

"Sean Peters!" Chris grinned, then let out a small sigh as she fluttered her hand over heart. "Sean Peters! I've been dying to meet him my whole life."

"Overrated," Evan said. "Dyes his hair. His muscles are most likely inflatable. I've heard he's impotent."

"Evan, Evan, give the man a break. It's tough being a legend."

"Yeah, you're right. Listen, you go ahead. I think I'd better leave."

"Leave?" She clutched his arm as all the joy went out of the evening.

"I hate Sean Peters. At least I do right now."

"But—"

"Look, I'm in a piss-poor mood and I'll do or say something to ruin your fun. Keep the jacket so you don't get cold." He detached her hand from his arm and rose from the bench. "I'll see you later. At the hotel."

"Evan—"

"Later, I promise."

He slipped away just before she heard a triumphant "There you are!" from Marla.

Chris squinted at Evan's retreating back, swallowed down a sudden sense of apprehension, and turned around to meet one of her life-long idols.

Chris heard a loud pounding on her door at three in the morning. Not that she was asleep. She'd had a couple of cups of coffee in Marla's kitchen, several glasses of water at the hotel, and two aspirin, but she was still feeling headachy and anxious. She threw on a robe and, holding her hand to her forehead, walked slowly from the bedroom into the sitting room, turning on a lamp before she opened the door.

Evan stood there, an elbow propped on the doorframe. His white shirt was rumpled and his face seemed drawn. In spite of his disheveled state, he still radiated tough, male sexiness, and Chris wondered again how one man could look so good, when he was obviously so miserable.

"Where have you been?" she asked.

"In my car, in the parking lot. Thinking."

"Well, come on in."

Pulling her robe more tightly to her, she walked over to an armchair and sat down, rubbing her temples with her fingertips.

Evan closed the door, followed her into the room, and stood in front of her. "Headache?"

"A whopper. I know, I drank too much. You don't have to tell me."

"I wasn't about to."

"Good." She sat back in the chair, tucked her legs up under her robe, and looked up at him. "I'm not feeling as witty or sparkling as I did at the party."

"I don't need you to be witty or sparkling. So, how did things go with Sean Peters?"

"I think I liked him better before I met him. I'm going to remember the Sean Peters who used to whip the bad guys and kiss the beautiful ladies in all those movies instead of the Sean Peters I met tonight, the one who has a sweaty handshake and kept fussing with the back of his head to make sure the obviously dyed hair was still combed over his bald spot."

Even with his mind on emotional overload, Evan appreciated Chris's sense of humor. He smiled at her, and she smiled back. No, there was no danger of her going Hollywood, and he'd been a fool for even thinking that. "So," he said, perching on the arm of the sofa next to her chair, "I take it you're not going to run away with him?"

"Nope."

"But you are going to leave. In the morning, I mean."

"Yep."

"What if I ask you to stay?"

The question threw her, he could tell. "Excuse me?"

"What if I asked you to get the kids and come back out here and live with me?"

Chris gripped the arms of the overstuffed chair and stared at him for a moment with an expression of disbelief. "Is this some kind of test question? *Are* you asking me?"

"Yes. I've been thinking about it, and it's the only solution I could come up with." He tunneled his fingers through his hair, muttered a couple of choice curses, and shook his head. "Tell me, do you think I could have expressed that one any worse? I'm really making a mess of this, aren't I?"

Chris shook her head slowly. How troubled, how conflicted Evan was. And how he hated her seeing it. He was of the old school—the archetypal cowboy, the strong man who suffers silently. And suffers alone.

"Evan," she said. "I don't know what to say."

"*You* don't know what to say? How the hell do you think I feel? I make my living with words, and I can't dredge up the right ones. Not tonight. All I know is that I can't bear the thought of losing you." His incredible turquoise eyes reflected confusion and disquiet. "I want to give it a try. I mean it, Chris. Go back to Loman, pack up the kids, and come back here. Will you?"

Chris felt drained. These days and nights with Evan, the unburdening of her life story, the party, the ups and downs she'd been experiencing all day. She was absolutely exhausted. She looked at him for a while before speaking. "You know, only a few hours ago I would have given an arm to hear you say that. But"—she shook her head slowly—"something's wrong here. This whole conversation seems off the wall. It's not enough just to 'give it a try.' I need more than a try, Evan."

"You want a guarantee? I don't know if I can give you that."

"No, not a guarantee." She rubbed her eyes with her fingers, then looked up at him again. His body was so tense, he looked ready to spring from the couch. "Let's be practical for a moment. If I didn't have kids, maybe I could take a chance. But I do have kids and they need a father."

He nodded. "Yeah."

"So, you would have to spend some time getting to know each other before I would even think about tearing them away from their friends, their home. But forget about the kids for a moment. You and I have been together for, what, four days? I think we both need some time to make sure."

He scowled and looked down at his lap.

"Evan," she said wearily, "I've spent most of my life looking for a place where I was wanted. Where I belonged. I would like to find that with you. But right now there's a kind of desperate bargain you want to strike, not because you want me, but because you're afraid to lose me." She shook her head slowly. "I don't think that's enough, Evan. I'm sorry. It's not enough."

"What will be enough?"

She allowed her gaze to roam his face, feeling as though she needed to memorize it. "I'm not sure. Trust, I guess. I already trust you, but you can't say the same, not yet. You're still not sure that I won't leave you the way all the other women have."

His face was stern. "That's right. If you leave me tomorrow, how do I know I'll ever see you again?"

"Some things you have to take on faith. And if you don't have faith in someone—in me, in yourself too, I guess—well, no amount of words will make it come out right." She raised her hands, then let them drop back into her lap.

Evan searched her face. For what? she wondered silently. A sign? A guarantee?

A miracle?

Finally, he spoke. "You know something, Chris?" he said with a small, sad smile. "I have the strangest feeling that we've changed places."

"What do you mean?"

"When I met you, you were scared and full of secrets. And weighted down from all the responsibilities you were carrying. And now you've let go of your secrets and it's like you're ten years younger. You're not scared anymore, are you? You're confident now . . . free, really. A whole other person."

Yes, she thought with a shock of recognition. That metamorphosis she'd felt earlier looking in the mirror, that was what he was talking about. He was right; there had been an enormous change. "And I owe it all to you."

"No. I just happened along when you were ready."

"You're wrong, you know. It wouldn't have happened with anyone else. You rescued me."

"Is that what you think?" He shrugged dispiritedly. "If you want to believe that, fine. But somewhere in there we changed places. I used to feel free and confident. I used to be fearless—or I thought I was anyhow. And now," he said quietly, "I'm scared to death."

She stopped breathing for a moment, unbearably moved by his admission. How difficult it must have been for him to say that. "Evan?"

"Yes?"

"I know all about being scared."

"Yeah, you do, don't you? But you also know how to walk through it, how to hope, how to— What was it you said? How to believe in things that don't seem possible? I haven't learned that yet. Do you think I can?"

"Knowing me as you do, you know my answer. Of course you can."

"I would like to feel that way. I hope I will someday."

He rose from where he'd been sitting on the arm of the couch and stood in front of her. She lifted her head to look at him at the same moment he bent over, and they smiled at each other, then kissed. A nice, soft, sweet kiss, one that answered no questions and decided no futures, but that touched her deeply.

Evan cupped her cheek in his hand and gazed at her for a silent moment. There was so much sadness, so much pain in his eyes, she wanted to reach out and comfort him with all her being. But she stayed where she was because she knew that was the way it had to be.

"You have an early plane," he said, "so I'd better go. I can't ask you to wait for me, Chris, because I don't know how long this is going to take. But I'm going to try to be what you need me to be so that we can be together."

"Evan, all I need you to be, all I want you to be, is you. And to love me."

He nodded, then slowly walked over to the door. With his hand on the doorknob he turned to face her for the last time, one of his small smiles curving his mouth. "I'm going to miss you like crazy. Have a safe trip."

Evan stood on his mountain and regarded the vista stretched out before him. He hadn't been up there in weeks. A steady rain was falling and the overcast sky nearly obscured the light from the rising sun. Gray, all gray. The ocean, the sky, the cars. Even the headlights were muted, caught up in the mist.

Words swirled around in his head, bits and pieces of dialogue from the script he'd been writing. Images flashed through his mind's eye like someone shuffling stills from a motion picture:

Chris at eighteen, staring out through a windshield at the vast black night, her hand lying protectively over her slightly rounded belly.

Chris in a stark white hospital room, gazing down in grief at the lifeless form of her husband on the bed.

Chris meeting the eyes of a helpless woman lying on the ground of a convenience store, and sending a message of encouragement even as the barrel of a gun is being pressed to her own head.

And Chris staring at Evan's back as he walks out of her hotel room, her expression as bleak as the feeling in his gut.

He'd been like this for nearly a month—driven, obsessed, to get the script done. No sleep, no company, nothing but the words and scenes that poured out of his head like a flood. He knew it was some of the best stuff he'd ever written, but that had nothing to do with anything.

He'd said he would miss her, and he hadn't been wrong.

What he hadn't realized was how much she'd taken over his soul. Even this place, the top of the mountain that he'd used to think of as his, was forevermore seared in his memory as the place where Chris unfolded her life story, the place they'd watched the sun set, the place they'd embraced passionately. His and Chris's place.

How he missed her! It was as though a limb were gone, as though he'd lost some part of himself.

He paid no attention to the rain dripping on his clothes and hair, the droplets catching in his lashes like tears.

"Chris," he said aloud, to no one. "Chris."

And as the words left his mouth and joined the air around him, he swore he could sense her, her humorous, loving presence. He felt surrounded by her, strangely warmed even in the chilled dampness of the morning.

And some more ice melted inside, the way it had been melting since he and Chris had been together for those magical four days. He'd carried that coldness in the center of his being, it seemed, forever. But no longer. Finally, something glowing and alive—something liquid—was taking its place, a sensation more real and more life-affirming than he'd ever experienced in his life.

Now he knew for sure. Chris was part of him, and he was part of her.

The struggle was over.

"Hi, Mrs. McConnell."

"Hi, Leon."

Chris closed the door to the principal's office and walked down the hallway, automatically nodding and saying hello to other teachers and children along the way. But her mind wasn't really present.

She'd done it. She'd told the principal she wouldn't be back next year. Just as she'd told Dora that morning that she'd be taking the kids and moving by next summer. When asked where, Chris had said she didn't know, just somewhere else, somewhere with an ocean nearby.

Dora had fought her, then cried. Chris had cried too and told the older woman that wherever they wound up living, Dora would be welcome. Dora had accused Chris of returning from her trip to L.A. a different person, and Chris had acknowledged the truth in that statement. One month ago she'd given up her secrets and their effect on her existence.

She'd also fallen in love, but that part of the story didn't yet have an outcome.

She hadn't heard a word from Evan, and wept herself to sleep most nights with missing him. She wondered how he was and how he was getting along. She wondered if she'd ever see him again.

She made her way out to the school yard. All around her, children were playing and running and laughing. She loved the sounds, and she loved teaching; she did it well. Whatever her new destination, she would teach there.

The bell rang, signaling the end of the morning exercise break. Children rushed by her, running back into the small brick building.

"Hello, Mrs. McConnell."

"Hello, Billy."

"Hi, Mrs. McConnell."

"Sarah, Candy."

In a matter of a few minutes the school yard was empty. This was Chris's free period and she chose to spend this time alone instead of in the teachers' lounge.

She walked over to the swings and sat down in one. Brown leaves blew through the school yard and she kicked at a couple by her feet. The day was windy and overcast, and she was glad she'd worn her heavy coat. Closing her eyes, Chris twisted the swing back and forth and raised her face to the sky. The faint smell of apples in the air reminded her that Thanksgiving was almost upon them. Where would she be at Thanksgiving next year?

"Hello, Mrs. McConnell."

Her heart thudded to a stop, then jump-started again. She looked up to see a pair of eyes the color of the ocean. The familiar crinkly sun and laugh lines seemed less deep somehow now that the hot months had passed. And the face—Evan's face—was different from what she remembered. Less shuttered.

He was dressed in familiar fashion—faded jeans, scuffed boots. His only nod to the weather was an unzipped Windbreaker over his T-shirt. His hair still hadn't been cut and was now longer and shaggier than ever. And yes, he was as mesmerizing, as sexy, as ever.

Her pulse started racing again, and she tried to tamp down the excitement his presence caused. "You shouldn't sneak up on a person while she's on a swing," she said with a smile. "I might have taken a tumble."

"Kids fall off swings every day. Most of them survive."

"But their bones and heads are softer."

"No one is softer than you."

Oh, she thought, and knew that if she'd had any expectations of forgetting this man, she was a total fool.

"No comeback, huh?" One side of his mouth quirked up, and he walked around her so that he was behind her. "Hold on," he said, then brought the swing back and let her go.

Chris gave a whoop of surprise. Evan pushed her again, until she was swinging high in the air, the way she used to as a child.

"Marla's going to be in a movie," Evan said, pushing her again. "A movie movie, not a TV movie. She's playing Gwen in *Second Impulse*."

Higher and higher she went, the feeling of freedom rushing through her bloodstream. "I read the book. It's junk, but it's a good role for her."

"That's what she thinks." He raised his voice so she could hear it over the wind in her ears. "And she's crowing with happiness."

"I can hear her now!"

Evan moved over to the side of the swings. Propping a hand on one of the steel poles, he followed her progress with his eyes. "The script is done."

"That was fast." As Chris passed him on her upward journey, she laughed out loud once again. Just a little higher, she thought, and she could fly.

"And it will never get made."

"Why not?" Chris stopped pumping and let the swing's momentum lessen.

"Most actors feel that working in television is second-rate. If they get a chance to break into *real* movies, they jump. Marla's been given the chance, so your story has been put on the back burner. By the time she's finished filming, it'll be a year from now, and you'll be last year's news."

Chris dragged her feet to make the swing come to a stop, realizing that her reaction to Evan's news was mixed.

Evan lowered himself onto the swing next to hers. "I thought you'd be glad."

"Well, I am, of course. I never wanted the thing filmed in the first place. I get to keep my privacy, and I've already gotten the money. But I don't know, all that effort, all that time spent. All your hard work. It seems a shame to waste it."

He shrugged. "It won't be the first time. The script is good. Maybe you'll read it sometime."

"I'd love to."

"I thought you'd be relieved. Weren't you worried about someone digging around in your past?"

"I guess I'm not so worried anymore. I made some mistakes, but I was just a kid." She smiled. "I thought it was time I let myself off the hook."

"I'm glad. Do Brian and Lisa know anything?"

"Some of it. What they can handle anyway. And as they grow older and can handle more, I'll tell them more." She rested her head against the thin chain that attached the swing to the crossbar and gazed at him. Oh, how good it was to see him again.

"Enough about me," she said. "Tell me about you. How have you been?"

"Lonely."

"Yeah, I know what you mean."

He smiled at her, not the way he usually smiled, as though he really didn't want to, but with an almost youthful openness that she had never seen in him before. "Hi," he said softly.

"Hi yourself."

Evan reached over and stroked Chris's cheek with a finger, then dropped his hand to his lap. Her skin was still like powder. "A funny thing happened while I was working on the script."

"And what was that?"

"A kind of . . . transformation. I was writing the story of a frightened, lonely woman who was also incredibly brave. I don't mean brave on the night someone stuck a gun to her head; it started earlier than that. She was given nothing—I mean, *nothing*, no name, no family, no support, not even any love—and managed to become a wonderful person anyway. Made something of herself, had kids, got a job. Had values and a work ethic and a contagious sense of joy. That woman became my hero."

A flush rose on Chris's cheeks, and she waved a weak, protesting hand in the air. "Stop it, Evan. Don't."

Evan wasn't ready to stop. This was too important to allow modesty to get in the way. "And I thought, damn, if she can rise above all that damage, why the hell can't I? And when I thought it, it started to happen. It was as if I were receiving a transfusion or something. From you. A little of your bravery, your optimism." He grinned. "Not a lot, mind you, but just enough to make the glass look a little less empty. My hero. By the way, you don't mind if I say hero instead of heroine, do you?"

"Really, Evan."

He grabbed the chain that held her swing and shook it gently. "It's all right, you know, for you to be my hero. It doesn't have to change anything between us."

"But that's how I feel about you," she said, her large gray eyes earnest as they met his. "All those times, rescuing me from Marla, and the crowd at the fair. Listening to me, to all that pain. Providing a safe place for me to purge all the secrets, to let down, to stop all the lying. Dear God, Evan, if anyone is a hero, it's you!"

He regarded her steadily, then nodded. He felt terrific. "We're pretty special, aren't we?"

"I guess we are."

They locked gazes for a little while longer, and Chris realized that the tightness in her chest—a tightness she'd been carrying for a month—had loosened up and disappeared, and she hadn't even noticed. The wind blew a little harder, and the smell of apples blended with the odor of leaves burning somewhere nearby.

Evan spoke first. "Buster says hello, by the way."

"How is Buster? And your house? And everyone in L.A.?"

"About the same."

"Warped and corrupted?"

"Human. Which a certain female philosopher once told me is both the good news and the bad."

"I see." And she did. She sighed. "I like what I'm hearing."

He reached into his back pocket and brought out a crumbled tissue. "I hope you like this too," he said, handing it to her.

As she held it, she realized there was something inside. Her heart started thumping again, loudly this time, as she separated the thin sheets of paper. There appeared a beautiful antique ring, gold with diamonds and seed pearls. She held it up and studied it through the sheen of tears that had sprung to her eyes. "Oh, Evan, this is beautiful."

"I hope you'll wear it. I've, uh, made a few plans. Care to hear them?"

"All right."

"I thought I'd hang around for a while."

"In Loman?"

He nodded. "Get to know the kids, get them to trust me, get you to trust me, get you to marry me."

Her mouth dropped open. All she could do was stare at him.

"Then, after a honeymoon, which will be your choice of anyplace in the world, I thought we could pack you all up and move you to my place. There's plenty of room."

"Dora too?"

His face fell. "Oh. Is she part of the deal?"

Chris bit back her laughter at the unhappy expression on his face. "No. Don't worry, she wouldn't leave here. But she will want to visit."

"I'll be tied up at the studio when she does."

They grinned at each other again. Then Evan took

her hand in his and squeezed it, and suddenly she felt overwhelmed by all the emotion in the air around them. Gazing down at the ring she was holding, she shook her head in wonder. "Such a lot of plans."

"I haven't finished."

Her head jerked up. "There's more? Boy, for the strong, silent type, you sure are verbal today."

With a brisk movement Evan fell to one knee in front of Chris. He took the hand he was holding and held it to his heart. "Chris," he said.

"What?"

"*Will* you marry me?"

"Yes."

"Whew. Good. Do you think you might want another child? Maybe two?"

She took about three seconds to consider it. "I could probably be talked into it."

"I'm glad. Because I want to be part of a family. I need that in the center of my life. I need you in the center of my life."

"That was some powerful transfusion I gave you."

His mouth quirked up. "More powerful than you can imagine." His expression turned serious again, and if she didn't know better, she would have thought there was a little moisture in his eyes.

"The thing is," he said softly, "I love you. I love you with every fiber of my being."

The tears in her eyes brimmed over and splashed down her cheeks. She was unbearably moved, unbearably happy. "Evan Stone," she said. "I believe you. I believe you do love me. Which is awfully convenient, as I happen to love you very much."

"Still?"

"Never stopped. Never will."

"I'm going to hold you to that."

"Please do. Forever."

Then Evan took her in his arms, there in the school yard, near the swings, with the leaves swirling around their feet, and Chris felt safe and warm and whole for the first time in her life.

THE EDITOR'S CORNER

Wrap up your summer in the most romantic way with the four upcoming LOVESWEPTs. Chivalry is alive and well in these love stories, so get ready for the most delicious thrills as each of the heroines finds her knight in shining armor.

Beloved for stories that weave heartbreak and humor into a tapestry of unforgettable romance, Helen Mittermeyer opens this month with **DYNASTY JONES,** LOVESWEPT #754. She is beautiful, spirited, a flame-haired angel whose lips promise heaven, but Aaron Burcell has to discover why his missing racehorse is grazing in Dynasty Jones's pasture! Honeysuckle Farm has been her sanctuary until Aaron breaches the walls that keep her safe from sorrow. Dynasty awakens every passionate impulse Aaron has ever felt, makes him want to slay dragons, but he must make her believe he will not betray her trust. Immerse yourself in this moving and tender tale of a love that heals with sweet and tender fire by the ever-popular Helen Mittermeyer.

Catch **ROGUE FEVER**, LOVESWEPT #755 by Jan Hudson. Long legs in dusty jeans, eyes shaded by a cowboy hat, Ben Favor looks every inch a scoundrel—and Savanna Smith feels his smile as a kiss of fire on her skin! She'd come to the sleepy Mexican town to trace a con man, but her search keeps getting sidetracked by a mesmerizing devil who makes her burn, then fans the flames. Savanna is the kind of woman a man will walk through fire for, but Ben will have to battle charging bulls and bad guys just to call this teasing temptress his. Award-winning Jan Hudson escorts you south of the border where the smart and sassy heroine always gets her man.

No city sizzles like New Orleans in Faye Hughes' **GOTTA HAVE IT**, LOVESWEPT #756. Once he'd been the most notorious jewel thief in the world, stealing from the rich for charity's sake, but now Remy Ballou insists he's gone straight—and Michael Ann O'Donnell fears for the legendary gems she's been hired to protect! His rogue's grin has haunted her dreams, while memories of his caresses still heat her blood. His words make her burn and his touch makes her shiver, but will the pirate who captured her soul long ago bind his heart to hers forever, or vanish in the shadows of the night? Find out in this steamy, sultry love story from Faye Hughes.

Debra Dixon explores the dangerous passions that spark between dusk and dawn in **HOT AS SIN**, LOVESWEPT #757. Emily Quinn is on the run, desperate to disappear before anyone else loses his life to save hers—and Gabe is her only hope! Tempted by her mystery, he agrees to help her evade her pursuers, but hiding a woman whose nightmares draw him into the line of fire awaken yearnings in his own secret heart. Once Gabe becomes more than a safe place to run, Emily strives to show him that forever will not be long enough. Let Debra Dixon lead you through this darkly sensual and exquisitely potent story about risking everything for love.

Happy reading!

With warmest wishes,

Beth de Guzman

Shauna Summers

Beth de Guzman

Senior Editor

Shauna Summers

Associate Editor

P.S. Watch for these spectacular Bantam women's fiction titles coming in September: With **LORD OF THE DRAGON**, Suzanne Robinson, one of the reigning stars of historical romance, presents her latest captivating love story in which a willful beauty and a vengeful knight cross swords; winner of the Catherine Cookson Prize for Fiction, Susanna Kearsley debuts as a spectacular new talent with **MARIANA**, a suspenseful tale of time travel that may be one of the most hauntingly beautiful love stories of the year. See next month's LOVESWEPTs for a preview of these enticing novels. And immediately following this page, look for a preview of the wonderful romances from Bantam that are *available now!*

Don't miss these extraordinary books
by your favorite Bantam authors

On sale in July:

DEFIANT
by Patricia Potter

STARCROSSED
by Susan Krinard

BEFORE I WAKE
by Terry Lawrence

DEFIANT

by "master storyteller"*
Patricia Potter

Only the desire for vengeance had spurred Wade Foster on, until the last of the men who had destroyed his family lay sprawled on the dirt. Now, badly wounded, the rugged outlaw closed his eyes against the pain . . . and awoke to the tender touch of the one woman who could show him how to live—and love—again.

"He'll be all right now, won't he?" her son asked.

Mary Jo nodded. "I think so. At least, I think he'll live. I don't know about that arm."

Jeff frowned. "Do you think he might be a lawman?"

"No," she said gently, "I don't think so."

"He wore his gun tied down."

"A lot of men wear their guns tied down."

"Did he say anything to you?"

She shook her head. She hated lying to her son, but she didn't want to tell him his new acquaintance had so coldly said he'd killed three men.

"Maybe he's a marshal. Or an army scout. He was wearing Indian beads."

"I don't think so, Jeff," she said. "He could just be a drifter."

"Then why did someone shoot him? Did he say?"

She shook her head, telling herself it wasn't a lie.

* *Rendezvous*

Wade Foster hadn't explained exactly why he'd been shot.

"Can I go see him?"

"I think he needs a little privacy right now," Mary Jo said. "But as soon as those biscuits are done, you can take some in and see if he can eat them."

Jeff was scuffing his shoes on the floor, waiting impatiently for the biscuits. She sought a way to expel some of that energy. "Why don't you get some wood for the fireplace?"

He nodded, fetched his oilcloth slicker, and disappeared out the door, eager for some action, even if it was only doing chores. She was hoping there would be a school next year; currently, there weren't enough families to support one, and she'd been teaching him herself from the few books she'd been able to find.

She stirred the broth as she kept her ears open for sounds beyond her bedroom door. Wade Foster should be finished with his personal needs now. He would need a wash and a shave.

She'd occasionally shaved her husband. It was one of the few personal things he'd enjoyed having done for him. But she hesitated to offer that service to the stranger. It had been an intimate thing between her and her husband; they had even occasionally ended in bed, though he usually preferred night for lovemaking. In some ways, he had been prudish about lovemaking, feeling there was a time and place for it, while Mary Jo thought any place or time was right between husband and wife as long as the desire was there.

The thought brought a hot blush to her cheeks and a yearning to her womanly place. It had been nearly three years since she'd last been loved. Hard work had subdued the need but now she felt the rush of heat deep inside.

She shook her head in disgust at herself. She couldn't believe she was having such feelings for the first stranger that came limping along. Especially this stranger.

But she just plain couldn't get Wade Foster out of her mind, not those intense eyes, or that strong, lean body under her bedclothes. Perhaps because of his grief over his son. She'd known grief, but she had never lost a child. And she'd never seen a man so consumed by sorrow.

He was a very disturbing man in many ways and she was foolish to harbor him without checking with the law.

Perhaps when the storm ended, she would ride to town and make inquiries. If she could ford the stream. If—

The door banged open and Jeff plunged back inside, rain flying in with him. Jake stayed outside, barking frantically.

"Men coming, Ma," Jeff said. "A lot of them."

Is anyone after you?

I expect so.

Almost without thinking, she made a decision.

"Jeff, don't say anything about the stranger."

"Why?" It was his favorite question and she always tried to give him answers. This time she didn't know if she could.

She looked at her son, wondering what kind of lesson she was teaching him now. But she had to protect the man they'd rescued. She didn't understand why she felt so strongly about it but there it was.

She tried the truth. "I think he's in trouble but I don't think he's a bad man."

Jeff thought about the answer for a moment. It was *his* stranger after all. He had found him. Well, his dog Jake had found him. And Jake liked him. That made the stranger all right in his book.

He nodded.

Mary Jo hurried toward her bedroom, giving only a brief knock before entering without invitation.

Wade Foster was on the side of the bed, the sheet obviously pulled quickly in front of his privates. His face was drenched in sweat, the color pale, his lips clenched together.

"Men are coming," she voiced aloud. "Could be a posse."

He tried to stand but couldn't. He fell back against the pillow, swearing softly. "I don't want to bring you trouble."

"No one could know you're here. The rain would have erased any tracks," she said. "I'll turn them away."

He stared at her. "Why?"

"I don't know," she said frankly.

"I don't want you or the boy involved."

"We already are, Mr. Foster. Now just stay here and be quiet."

"I don't understand you."

Mary Jo smiled. "Not many people do."

A loud knocking came at the front door, accompanied by Jake's renewed barking. She wished she'd had time to hide Wade Foster, she would just have to make sure no one searched the house. Thank God, everyone in this area knew she was the widow of a Texas Ranger and the heir of another. She would be the last person suspected of harboring a fugitive.

Casting a reassuring look at Jeff, she hurried to

the door, opened it and faced the sheriff and six of her neighbors.

"A man was found dead, killed some four miles to the west," Sheriff Matt Sinclair said. "We're checking all the ranches and farms."

She gave him a warm smile. Since the day that she and Jeff had come to Cimarron Valley, Matt had been kind, attentive, and concerned that she was trying to run a ranch on her own. Others had been contemptuous.

"In this weather?" she asked.

"The dead man appears to be a miner from his clothing, though God only knows what he was doing here." He cleared his throat, then added reluctantly, "He was shot once in the leg and then in the throat at close range. Cold-blooded killing if I've ever seen one. Just wanted to alert everyone, check if they've seen any strangers around."

Mary Jo slowly absorbed the news. Wade Foster had tried to warn her but she hadn't been prepared for the details.

"Do you have any idea who did it?"

"That there's the devil of it," the sheriff replied. "No one's seen or heard anything. Could be just plain robbery, and the killer's long gone, but I want to be sure everyone's warned."

"Thank you," Mary Jo said.

"I don't like leaving a woman and kid alone," he said. "One of my men can stay with you, sleep in the barn."

Mary Jo shook her head. "My husband taught me to shoot as good as any man and I wouldn't be reluctant to do it," she said. "Jeff here is just as good. And Jake would warn us of any trespassers. But I thank you for the offer."

"Well, then, if everything's all right . . ." His voice trailed off.

"Thank you for coming by, Sheriff." Mary Jo knew she should offer them something, particularly coffee but it was too risky. She started to shut the door.

The sheriff added, "I'll send someone over every couple of days to check on you."

"No need."

"Just to make me feel better," he said with a slight smile.

Mary Jo tried to smile back, but couldn't. She felt terribly deceitful.

Tell him, something inside her demanded. Tell him about the murderer in your bed.

But no words came. She merely nodded her thanks. As she watched him and the others mount their horses and ride away, she wondered if she had just made the worst mistake of her life.

STARCROSSED
by Susan Krinard

At sixteen, Lady Ariane Burke-Marchand had loved Rook Galloway with all the passion and pain of unrequited love. It didn't matter that the handsome Kalian was separated from her by birth and caste and mansion walls. All she knew was that this exotic, mysterious creature called to her in ways she couldn't fathom or resist. But that was eight years ago, eight years before the deadly riots that pitted Marchand against Kalian and turned the man she worshiped into an enemy she loathed. . . .

Hudson ducked his head. "Permission to examine your hold and cabins, Lady Ariane. A formality."

A breath of wry laughter escaped her. "I'm not likely to be harboring fugitives on my ship, but I'll clear you."

She led him into the cargo hold and left him there, making her way through the final air lock and into the *d'Artagnan's* living quarters. There was something almost oppressive in the empty silence of the common room; even the cockpit seemed less a sanctuary than a cell.

Ariane shuddered and dropped into the padded

pilot's seat. *Don't think about it,* she commanded her-self. *At least this ship is something you can count on. Something certain.*

One by one she ran through the preflight rou-tines: checking the stardrive's balance for sublight flight, priming the ship's life support system, carrying out all the necessary tests. Again and again she forgot sequences that she knew by heart, remembering Rook's face.

Remembering how he had made her feel. . . .

No. Her fingers trembled on the keypad as she made the final entries. *You won't have to think about it much longer. It's over. It's out of your hands.*

But the memories remained while the ready lights came up on the control panel. She leaned back in the pilot's seat and passed her hand over her face.

Honor. All her life she'd been raised by the codes of the Espérancian Elite. Like the *d'Artagnan,* honor was solid and real. It had been insanity to doubt, to question. Duty and honor would send her back to Espérance. Honor would give her the courage to face a life of confinement. To accept.

To forget Rook Galloway.

Letting out a shuddering breath, she rose and be-gan to pace the tiny space of the cockpit restlessly. Hudson should have been done with his "routine" check by now. She flipped on the ship's intercom.

"Mr. Hudson? I'm ready for takeoff." She waited, tapping her fingers against the smooth console. "Mr. Hudson—"

"Here, Lady Ariane."

She whirled, with reflexes honed through years of training as a duelist. Hudson stood just inside the cockpit, a disruptor in his hand.

Aimed at her.

Her first impulse was to laugh. Hudson looked so deadly serious, his mouth set in a grim line that seemed so much at odds with his boyishly untouched face. But she clamped her lips together and balanced lightly on the balls of her feet, waiting.

"Did you find some—irregularity, Mr. Hudson?"

He moved another step closer. And another, until he was within touching distance. "Call for clearance to take off," he said, gesturing with the 'ruptor.

Ariane revised her first assumption. It wasn't what she had supposedly done; Hudson had simply gone crazy.

"I know—how it must be, Mr. Hudson. Alone here, far from home—you want to go back home, is that it? To Liberty?"

He stared at her, light blue eyes shadowed beneath his uniform cap. "Liberty," he repeated.

Considering the best way to move, Ariane tensed her muscles for action. "You must feel trapped here, so far from home. After what we saw . . . I understand. But—"

His smile vanished. "Trapped," he said softly. "What do you know about being trapped, Lady Ariane?" His voice had gone very deep and strange. "Call the tower for clearance. Now."

For the briefest instant Hudson's eyes flickered to the console behind her, and Ariane moved. She darted at Hudson, whirling like a dancer in the ancient way her family's old Weapons Master had taught her as a girl. She might as well have attacked a plasteel bulkhead. Powerful arms caught and held her; the 'ruptor's muzzle came up against her head.

Shock held her utterly still for one blinding instant. Hudson's hand burned on her arm like the bitter cold of space.

"I don't have much to lose, Lady Ariane," Hudson said softly. "You'll call for clearance. Everything is perfectly—normal."

She considered fighting again; to put the *d'Artagnan* in a starjacker's hands was unthinkable.

But there was far more at stake. Marchand honor and Marchand interest demanded her safe return, to wed Wynn Slayton by inviolable contract that would bind their families forever. Her death now would gain nothing at all.

Clenching her teeth, Ariane hailed the prison port and made the final, in-person request for clearance. The bored officer's voice on the other end of the commlink never altered; her own was perfectly steady as she acknowledged her clearance to lift.

Abruptly Hudson let her go. "Very good," he murmured. "Take her up."

Ariane thought quickly as she dropped into the pilot's seat, Hudson breathing harshly over her shoulder. *He's only a boy. He can't know much about Caravel-class starships. . . .*

Her hand hovered just above the control stick. It shouldn't be too difficult to fool the young guard, make it seem as if they were leaving the system. And then—

Warm fingers feathered along her shoulder and slid under the thick hair at the base of her neck. "Oh no, Lady Ariane. It won't be so easy this time."

Her throat went dry as her hand fell from the console. Abruptly he let her go, stepping away. She turned in the seat to look up at the man who stood over her.

And he *changed*. As if he were made of something other than mere human flesh he began to change:

slowly, so slowly that at first she didn't realize what she was seeing.

The young man's softness vanished, cheekbones and hollows and sharp angles drawn forth from Hudson's unremarkable face. Sandy hair darkened in a slow wave under the uniform cap. An old scar snaked over skin tanned by relentless heat.

The eyes were the last to change. Blue faded, warmed, melted into copper.

Rook's eyes.

They held hers as he swept off his cap, freed the dark hair that fell to his shoulders.

The man who stood before her wore the tailored uniform of a Tantalan guard as a hellhound might wear a collar. A wild beast crouched on the deck of the *d'Artagnan*.

A Kalian.

Reaction coursed through her, numbing her hands and stopping her breath.

"*Mon Dieu*," she whispered. "You."

BEFORE I WAKE
by Terry Lawrence

*Loveswept star Terry Lawrence is an extraordinary story-
teller whose novels sizzle with irresistible wit and high-
voltage passion. Now, she weaves the beloved fairy tale*
Sleeping Beauty *into a story so enthralling it will keep
you up long into the night. . . .*

She came clean. "Gabe, I simply must apologize. I
have something I'm sorry to tell you."

"You're married."

She croaked a laugh. "Ha ha. No." Her flippant
wave fooled no one. She wasn't good with men. Actually, she wasn't bad. She'd had relationships. Some of
them had proceeded all the way to bed and *then*
they'd fallen apart. "We taped you."

"You what?"

She swung around in her chair and retrieved the
black plastic box. When she swung back he was still
smiling. This time a cautious glint lurked in his blue
eyes.

"The night tech on duty in the sleep lab the evening you were here filmed you sleeping. It's common
practice, we do it all the time."

"Do you?"

"I'm apologizing because we didn't have your permission."

"Ah." He took the tape from her, his tapering fingers touching hers. Their gazes met and held. "Did you watch it?"

Where were those stacks of folders when she needed a place to hide? "A little. You seemed to have slept well."

"Like the dead." One side of his mouth curved up.

She'd never noticed the way his brows arched, like Gothic windows in a gloomy cathedral. He had an air of the fallen angel about him, the devilish rogue, the lost soul. He'd referred to himself as something of the sort, though she couldn't remember exactly how.

She felt light-headed. The atmosphere was too close. She'd been lost in his eyes too long. She needed air. She could handle this. She rose, her legs shaking, and edged her way around her desk. From there to the window seemed like miles.

He turned his head, following her with his eyes. His body seemed unnaturally still. Hers seemed unbearably energized. Her pulse skittered through her veins. Her breath skimmed in and out of her lungs.

"So you've been sleeping better," she said, making conversation, gripping the window frame. The wood was ancient, the paint peeling and dry. She shoved. The frame didn't budge. Pressing her wrists against the chilly glass, she tried again. Her breath frosted the pane. She inhaled the musty odor of rotting wood.

Gabe reached around her from behind. She froze, her breath trapped in her lungs. He rested his thumbs on her knuckles, splaying his hands on either side of hers. In one sharp move he thrust the window upward. The wood screeched like an angry bird.

In the ensuing silence, traffic noise rose from the street below. Cold air flooded the room, slithering into the gaps of her coat, shocking her with its icy fingers. She turned with great effort. Sagging against the sill, she gripped the splintery wood on either side of her thighs.

Gabe rested his hands on her shoulders. "Shana."

His grogginess was long gone. A feral alertness sharpened his features. He lingered over her name like a starving man over a meal. His lids lowered. He concentrated on her lips. She longed to taste his.

She fought for air, for sense. She couldn't do this. Whirling in the tight circle of his arms, she flattened her palms against the glass. They instantly formed a misty outline, ten fingers clutching thin air.

His fingers closed over her wrists like talons capturing her hammering pulse. His thumbs curled into her damp palms. Mingled breaths frosted the pane, blotting out the world outside.

"Please," she panted. She was slipping, her will ebbing with every weak breath. This wasn't right. She pressed her cheek to the window, letting the mind-clearing reality of bitter cold bite into it. The chill penetrated her clothing, pebbling her breasts. The hard line of the sill pressed across her thighs.

An eerie incongruous warmth whispered across her face. His breath. He lifted her hair off her neck. She tried to protest. Her lips barely parted. "I can't believe we're doing this again."

"Believe."

"We can't."

"We can."

And don't miss these spellbinding romances from Bantam Books, on sale in August:

LORD OF THE DRAGON
by Suzanne Robinson

"An author with star quality . . . spectacularly talented."
—*Romantic Times*

MARIANA
by Susanna Kearsley

Winner of the Catherine Cookson Prize for fiction

To enter the sweepstakes outlined below, you must respond by the date specified and follow all entry instructions published elsewhere in this offer.

DREAM COME TRUE SWEEPSTAKES

Sweepstakes begins 9/1/94, ends 1/15/96. To qualify for the Early Bird Prize, entry must be received by the date specified elsewhere in this offer. Winners will be selected in random drawings on 2/29/96 by an independent judging organization whose decisions are final. Early Bird winner will be selected in a separate drawing from among all qualifying entries.

Odds of winning determined by total number of entries received. Distribution not to exceed 300 million.

Estimated maximum retail value of prizes: Grand (1) $25,000 (cash alternative $20,000); First (1) $2,000; Second (1) $750; Third (50) $75; Fourth (1,000) $50; Early Bird (1) $5,000. Total prize value: $86,500.

Automobile and travel trailer must be picked up at a local dealer; all other merchandise prizes will be shipped to winners. Awarding of any prize to a minor will require written permission of parent/guardian. If a trip prize is won by a minor, s/he must be accompanied by parent/legal guardian. Trip prizes subject to availability and must be completed within 12 months of date awarded. Blackout dates may apply. Early Bird trip is on a space available basis and does not include port charges, gratuities, optional shore excursions and onboard personal purchases. Prizes are not transferable or redeemable for cash except as specified. No substitution for prizes except as necessary due to unavailability. Travel trailer and/or automobile license and registration fees are winners' responsibility as are any other incidental expenses not specified herein.

Early Bird Prize may not be offered in some presentations of this sweepstakes. Grand through third prize winners will have the option of selecting any prize offered at level won. All prizes will be awarded. Drawing will be held at 204 Center Square Road, Bridgeport, NJ 08014. Winners need not be present. For winners list (available in June, 1996), send a self-addressed, stamped envelope by 1/15/96 to: Dream Come True Winners, P.O. Box 572, Gibbstown, NJ 08027.

THE FOLLOWING APPLIES TO THE SWEEPSTAKES ABOVE:

No purchase necessary. No photocopied or mechanically reproduced entries will be accepted. Not responsible for lost, late, misdirected, damaged, incomplete, illegible, or postage-die mail. Entries become the property of sponsors and will not be returned.

Winner(s) will be notified by mail. Winner(s) may be required to sign and return an affidavit of eligibility/release within 14 days of date on notification or an alternate may be selected. Except where prohibited by law, entry constitutes permission to use of winners' names, hometowns, and likenesses for publicity without additional compensation. Void where prohibited or restricted. All federal, state, provincial, and local laws and regulations apply.

All prize values are in U.S. currency. Presentation of prizes may vary; values at a given prize level will be approximately the same. All taxes are winners' responsibility.

Canadian residents, in order to win, must first correctly answer a time-limited skill testing question administered by mail. Any litigation regarding the conduct and awarding of a prize in this publicity contest by a resident of the province of Quebec may be submitted to the Regie des loteries et courses du Quebec.

Sweepstakes is open to legal residents of the U.S., Canada, and Europe (in those areas where made available) who have received this offer.

Sweepstakes in sponsored by Ventura Associates, 1211 Avenue of the Americas, New York, NY 10036 and presented by independent businesses. Employees of these, their advertising agencies and promotional companies involved in this promotion, and their immediate families, agents, successors, and assignees shall be ineligible to participate in the promotion and shall not be eligible for any prizes covered herein. SWP 3/95

DON'T MISS THESE FABULOUS BANTAM WOMEN'S FICTION TITLES

On sale in July

DEFIANT
by PATRICIA POTTER
Winner of the 1992 *Romantic Times*
Career Achievement Award for Storyteller of the Year

Only the desire for vengeance had spurred Wade Foster on, until the last of the men who had destroyed his family lay sprawled in the dirt. Now, badly wounded, the rugged outlaw closed his eyes against the pain . . . and awoke to the tender touch of the one woman who could show him how to live—and love—again. ____ 56601-6 $5.50/$6.99

STAR-CROSSED
by nationally bestselling author SUSAN KRINARD

"Susan Krinard was born to write romance."
—New York Times *bestselling author Amanda Quick*

A captivating futuristic romance in the tradition of Johanna Lindsey, Janelle Taylor, and Kathleen Morgan. A beautiful aristocrat risks a forbidden love . . . with a dangerously seductive man born of an alien race. ____ 56917-1 $4.99/$5.99

BEFORE I WAKE
by TERRY LAWRENCE

"Terry Lawrence is a magnificent writer." —Romantic Times

Award-winning author Terry Lawrence is an extraordinary storyteller whose novels sizzle with irresistible wit and high-voltage passion. Now, she weaves the beloved fairy tale *Sleeping Beauty* into a story so enthralling it will keep you up long into the night. ____ 56914-7 $5.50/$6.99

Ask for these books at your local bookstore or use this page to order.

Please send me the books I have checked above. I am enclosing $____ (add $2.50 to cover postage and handling). Send check or money order, no cash or C.O.D.'s, please.

Name _____

Address _____

City/State/Zip _____

Send order to: Bantam Books, Dept. FN159, 2451 S. Wolf Rd., Des Plaines, IL 60018
Allow four to six weeks for delivery.

Prices and availability subject to change without notice. FN 159 7/95